TALENTED

THE ARC SERIES BOOK TWO

ALEXANDRA MOODY

For my sisters.

CHAPTER ONE

There is no fighting the cold fear that slithers down my spine. No going back to the protective depths of the fallout shelter I've spent a lifetime calling home. And no ignoring the stark reality of the new world that lies before me.

Hope City glimmers like a shining beacon below us. With its soaring glassy towers that capture the sunlight on their skin, the place sparkles like a handful of tiny diamonds in the light. It's better than anything I could have dreamed up, and such a far cry from the fallout shelter I've been taken from. I couldn't compare the two if I tried.

Despite my awe, I watch the sprawling metropolis with distrusting eyes. Thousands of people still live in a darkened world underground, with not even the slightest clue life has returned to the surface. Could this place really exist? It's too good to be true—it has to be.

Gord is quiet as he concentrates on carefully lowering the helicopter down towards the landing platform. His tense jaw and hardened expression reveal his focus is totally on the job at hand. I should be excited about flying through the skies and finally seeing the sun. I should feel ecstatic I'm so close to finding Sebastian. But seeing this secret city, finally knowing the truth after so many years in the dark, I feel nothing but fear.

Looking outside my window as we descend, I am confronted by the world that lies just beyond. Towers that had initially only been small, shiny spikes, off in the distance, loom over me. With their mighty reach, they leave only a hint of sky above us—a small square of blue, framed by the harsh outlines of the surrounding buildings.

One building is so close to us now the helicopter is reflected along its surface. My eyes travel down the windows that shimmer like molten liquid to the ground that draws closer. The concrete square we aim for is partially covered in shadow from the tall building nearest to us, with a thick yellow circle painted like a target on the ground.

My hands begin shaking, so I push them against my legs to still the quiver. I close my eyes and sit back in my seat, trying to relax.

As the helicopter touches down it jolts, throwing my body forward against the restraints across my chest. I grab hold of the edge of my seat and squeeze the material tightly.

I shouldn't be here.

A woman runs towards us across the helipad, ducking down low as she makes her way to my door. Her hair is a vibrant red under the sunshine, and her bright blue sundress billows as the helicopter propellers gust at her.

I want to ask Gord why she's wearing clothes from before impact, but my mouth goes dry and the words stick in my throat. A face appears at my door and the red-headed woman opens it.

'Hi Elle,' she says, pleasantly enough. 'Welcome to Hope. My name is Faye and I'm here to escort you to the reintegration centre.'

I can feel my head nodding, but the reaction feels disconnected from the rest of my body, which remains sitting rigidly in the seat. My eyes dart from the woman's face to Gord's. He gives me an encouraging nod, indicating I should follow this stranger.

'Go on...' he suggests, when I continue to hesitate.

My hands, still tight around the edge of the seat, begin to sweat and a wave of nausea hits me. I can't imagine myself leaving the safety of the chopper and the thought makes my breath run short and shallow.

'The sun's out, the air is fresh ... it's really beautiful out here,' Faye says.

I glance past her at the vibrant green trees in the garden that lines the far side of the helipad. Their leaves almost shimmer in the breeze, rising and falling as though taking part in some ancient dance from time long gone by. She's right, it is beautiful, but my lungs constrict, and I struggle to breathe easily as I try to process the fact I'm about to step out onto the surface.

I slowly take off my headset and place it carefully on the seat, my hands clearly shaking as I lay it down.

'Thank you,' I say to Gord.

He gives an easy wave of his hand. 'Anytime.'

The propellers are still rotating as I lower myself from the helicopter. They blow my hair everywhere and whip my dull grey clothes against my body. As my feet step down onto the solid ground, I hold my hair back from my face and look up to the blue sky far above. I close my eyes and take a deep breath in, tasting the crisp air that fills my lungs.

I've made it.

Once we're clear of the helicopter, it lifts off the ground and up into the air. I watch as it moves off into the distance and, when it disappears from sight, I feel very much alone again.

'Elle...'

'Yes?' I turn away from the sky to face Faye.

'If you'd like to come with me, we'll go inside now.' She indicates with one hand towards the large building that covers the helipad with its long shadow. It's smaller than the other skyscrapers we flew past to get here, but massive all the same, and the way it looms over us here on the ground it's all the more intimidating.

I am led to an entrance where two men in black suits stand with such rigid stature they couldn't be anything other than guards. Their faces are blank and they stare out at nothing in particular, but their bodies look wired, as though ready to pounce at a moment's notice.

Their presence here makes me nervous and I feel a wave of uncertainty. The men are so similar to the officials in the ARC. Is it safe to enter this building? Can I trust these complete strangers? Is there even any point in feeling apprehensive when I have no power but to do as I'm told?

I gave up any say I have in my life the second I swapped my blood sample so I could be taken. There really is nothing I can do now I've been brought here.

It's worth it, I remind myself. For Sebastian, it's worth it.

I pause by the door and glance back over my shoulder towards the helipad. The sun is warm, yet I have the smallest of goose bumps over my skin from the cool breeze that dances across my arms. It's refreshing in a way I could never have imagined and I don't want to go inside again so soon, but as the woman lightly touches my arm to guide me forward, I know I don't really have a choice.

I follow her through the revolving door and into a large foyer. Only two steps into the building and I can already tell this place is nothing like the ARC. Natural light streams in through large, floor-to-ceiling windows that reach up several stories high. The ceiling, far above, scoops upwards in a curve and the floor is covered in the shiniest cream marble tiles. Large screens flash pictures of the city across them. It looks beautiful, with green parks and lakes, bustling city streets and markets. It even shows footage of children playing a ball game on a large green oval.

Faye leads me to a locked door and punches in a code to let us in. I trail after her down a long corridor, and begin to lag further and further behind as I catch glimpses of different rooms from the open doorways. I hear the shortest snippets of conversations and the rumbling undercurrent of laughter in the rooms I pass. There's the constant beat of some music playing further down the corridor and as we walk past an open window I notice the sounds of the busy street just beyond it. This place is so alive. A hive of activity that buzzes in a way the ARC never could.

'Just in here Elle,' Faye says, leading me into a small office. The place looks like a bomb has hit it. There are endless mounds of files scattered all over the floor and tall stacks of paper, which reach for the ceiling from the desk. She rushes to one of the seats in the room and pulls some papers off it, setting them down on top of an already teetering tower that sits on her desk, before offering the chair out to me.

She sits down on the other side of the table and places the tablet she's been holding down in the only spare space on the desk. With a swift movement, she spins her chair around to face the back of the room and begins sifting through a stack of folders that sits there. While she's occupied I peer down at the screen. I find there's a document open with lots of writing and a picture of my face in the top corner of it. The sight of my picture on the screen makes my stomach drop.

'Now I swear I'd left the folder just here...' Faye mutters to herself, as she moves to search another pile.

I've never seen the photo before in my life and it looks fairly recent. How on earth did they get that? I shuffle to the edge of my seat to try and get a better look at what has been written below, but miss my opportunity as Faye turns back to me and picks the tablet back up.

'No matter,' she says, having failed to find the file she was after. 'I just have a few initial questions, so let's dive straight into it. Can you state your full name for me please?'

'Elle Winters.'

'You're seventeen. Correct?'

'Yes.'

'And your parents died on impact?'

My eyes had started to wander towards some of the papers on her desk and they reflexively jerk back to her face.

'Yes,' I respond, unable to understand why she would need to ask such a question.

'You have no blood relatives in the ARC or who have been taken?' she reiterates.

'That's correct.'

'And you never stayed with a host family for longer than five years?'

'No, never longer than four.' It's quite obvious she already knows all these answers, almost like she's going down a checklist and confirming its accuracy.

She nods and then begins tapping on her tablet.

'Why have I been brought here?' I ask.

'We'll answer that in your reintegration session...' she says, not looking up from her tablet.

'Then what will happen?'

'We'll also talk more about that in your reintegration session. What I can tell you is you're in luck,' she smiles and looks up from her tablet. 'We have a family available to take you in today. We will be placing you with them until you've become accustomed to your new life here. They will help you adjust, make sure you get to school and help you get some proper clothing from the refuse centre.' My eyes widen at the thought. 'Yes, you won't be wearing those greys anymore.'

She pulls open one of her desk drawers, takes something out and slides it across the desk towards me.

'Here's your new CommuCuff. I am assigned to your case and if you ever need to talk to someone about anything my username is programmed in as @FayeMasters. I know it can be hard to settle in, but we want the transition to be as easy as possible for you.'

I look down at my new cuff and hope spurs inside of me.

'These CommuCuffs aren't able to sync with those in the ARC,' she says, as though reading my thoughts. My shoulders slump, defeated. Even just one second of hoping I'd be able to contact Quinn, back in the ARC, is devastating to lose.

I clip the cuff onto my wrist, and shake and twist it around uncomfortably. It feels too big and doesn't sit as well as my old one did.

'You'll find this cuff's more advanced than the ones in the ARC,' Faye explains. 'Most importantly, they have especially advanced GPS capabilities, so you shouldn't be getting lost up here.'

She begins shuffling in her seat, like she's about to leave.

'Um ... before we go I have a question...' I say, as she moves to stand up.

'We really have to get you to your session,' she responds. She doesn't look like she wants to be answering my questions, but this may be my only chance.

'I ... I had a friend who was taken recently. His name's Sebastian Scott. I'd like to see him if possible.' I hold my breath, waiting for her response.

'The name doesn't ring a bell, sorry. We have so many people who come through here, it's hard to keep track...'

'But you'd have to remember him. He was only here a few weeks ago.' I say.

'Like I said, there are so many people who come through here and I'm not the only case manager.' She looks slightly concerned at my insistence.

'But we've barely had anyone taken in the last few years...'

She laughs in response and stands. 'Maybe from your facility,' she says.

'W-what do you mean?' I stutter back.

'You may not have realised this, but there isn't just one ARC. There are several dozen placed all over the world.'

'There are?' I ask, jumping forward in my seat.

'Yes.'

'Why haven't I ever heard of them before?' I ask.

She glances meaningfully at her CommuCuff. 'Look, you will have plenty of time for questions in the reintegration session, which we really need to leave for if you don't want to miss the introduction.'

'But—'

'I'm sorry Elle, but we're already running late.' She moves towards the door and pulls it open. I sigh and follow her out of the room. There may be time for questions, my only hope is they'll be willing to provide me with the answers I need.

CHAPTER TWO

Faye leads me down a long and seemingly endless corridor to the other end of the building and a room identified as 'Reintegration Room 2.' When we walk in I'm surprised to find several other kids waiting. They are all seated, looking towards the large floor-to-ceiling windows that take up a whole wall of the room. Their hushed murmurs abruptly stop and the room falls silent as we enter, with every head turning to watch us walk in.

I feel incredibly self-conscious as they stare at me. I try to appear like I haven't noticed the six sets of beady eyes that scrutinise my every movement, but it's difficult. Especially when it appears I'm the only one wearing the grey clothing from the ARC. I cross my arms over my chest as I move into the room, and try to ignore how the colour of my clothes feels even more dull than usual.

I am directed to take a seat next to one of the boys. He looks a few years younger and he smiles shyly at me as I take a seat. Now I'm closer, I see the black slacks and black top he's wearing are almost identical to my greys, but for the colour. I give him a slight nod and turn to look at the woman who stands in front of the window before us.

Her dark hair is pulled back tightly and she smooths her hands down the front of her suit pants before she begins. 'First off, I want to welcome you to Hope,' she says, giving us the smile of someone who's given that same 'welcome' smile countless times. It's completely lacking any real warmth.

'I'm in charge of helping people, like yourselves, become adjusted to your new home.'

I look at the other kids, waiting to feel a jolt of recognition, but I don't know a single one. From the looks on their faces this is all clearly new to them too. They're definitely not from my ARC, so at least Faye was telling the truth about the other fallout shelters. I'm struggling to wrap my mind around the idea and can't understand why they kept so many secrets from us. What reason could there possibly be?

Looking back to the woman, I notice the street behind her. The glass window acts as a clear barrier between us and the pavement outside. People are hurrying past, not even slightly interested in our group that sits just inside. I desperately hope to see Sebastian out there, but already I'm beginning to feel a building worry about how many people there are here and how difficult it will be to find him.

'As you will all be aware, you have been brought here because your blood test came back with a tainted reading. Despite what you have been told in the ARC, this is not something to be feared, rather something to be embraced. You may have been called tainted in the ARC, but what you really are is something special and quite unique.

'You have all been given a gift. The gradual exposure to Lysartium over the years has slowly changed you and a mutation in your genes has allowed for the development of talents. None of you are tainted. What you do have is unbounded potential to one day be *talented*.'

'What do you mean, talents?' one of the boys behind me interrupts. I turn in my chair to glance at him. He must be about fifteen and has flaming red hair that sticks out at all the wrong angles. He slouches down in his chair, attempting to appear like he doesn't care, and when he catches my eye he winks. I quickly look back to the front of the room.

'The mutation has allowed the human brain to develop in ways we only ever read about in science fiction. We have seen cases of increased memory, strength, speed, extrasensory perception ... really we are yet to see the limits of what humans are now capable of.'

'I'm fairly certain my memory is just as bad today as it was yesterday,' the same boy interrupts again, triggering several giggles from the younger girls in the group.

The woman eyeballs him, causing the room to go silent. Her upper lip almost curls as she responds. 'It is unlikely any of you will exhibit such talents yet. Your test results gave indication of only the slightest mutation and you have been assigned talent levels of five and below. As such, you will be placed in East Hope, where you will be given the opportunity to improve any talents you develop over time.'

I have so many questions for this woman, but I begin to worry about drawing attention to myself. If what she says is true, and I'm completely normal in a world filled with these 'talents,' I'm in big trouble.

'If you focus and work really hard on your talent, you may find yourself one of the lucky ones who get recruited to North Hope, where we have a special academy dedicated to the talented. The academy is extremely prestigious, so only those recruited are allowed in the north of the city.'

There are a few soft whispers at the mention of a special academy and even this woman, who struggles to appear enthused about welcoming us here, is excited by the prospect of recruitment.

'Why can't my mum come to the surface too?' one of the girls asks.

'Yeah, why doesn't anyone in the ARC know about the surface?' another joins in, as the other kids in the room speak up, agreeing.

'Unfortunately,' she raises her voice to be heard over the group, 'Hope is still very much in the early stages of development and we don't have the resources to provide for everyone from your respective

ARCs. Until we are able to set up more farming land for crops, we simply cannot support such an influx of people. Once those arrangements are in place, we will of course begin to relocate all ARC citizens above ground.'

'How come it's sunny here?' the boy beside me asks.

'Good question. If you go outside on a sunny day and look up to the sky, sometimes you will see a shimmer in the air, way up high. This is the protective shield that covers Hope, called The Sphere. It filters the air, deflecting the heavy dirt and grit away from the city. It was developed to aid with pollution before impact, but they've found a much better purpose for it now. Any other questions?'

I slowly raise my hand. 'How do we get in contact with old friends from the ARC who are on the surface?'

'That information is only available to immediate family. Anyone else?' she asks, with a quick, cursory glance around the room. 'If there are no other questions, we will start calling your names so we can escort you to your assigned accommodation.'

My stomach does an uneasy flip as she says this. I was told they'd arranged a family for me to stay with and I give a moment's thought to what the people will be like.

The woman calls out one of the girl's names and proceeds to lead her from the room. As soon as they've left, the other kids start talking in hushed whispers. I don't join them. Instead, I focus back on the people walking past the window. It's difficult to block the others out though with words like 'tainted,' and 'talented,' being thrown around.

'Do you miss your family?' the boy next to me asks.

'No.' I turn to look at him. 'Why?'

He tilts his head and watches me closely. 'You just looked sad is all. It's okay, you know, to miss them...'

For the first time I notice his red-rimmed, puffy eyes. He's not the only one. Several of the others look like they've been crying and one of the girls is still wiping at the tears silently trickling down her cheeks.

'I'm not upset,' I assure him.

He nods in response, as though only to placate me, and quickly changes the subject. 'What do you think of everything she said?'

Hoping he gets the hint, I fold my arms and turn back to look out the window. No one has walked past in a little while now, so it's difficult to look immersed in the world outside when there's nothing going on out there.

From my peripheral vision, I notice the boy's shoulders slouch as he looks away. It's better if we don't talk. I need to keep to myself if I'm to protect the truth about how I came to be on the surface.

When my name is finally called there is only one other kid waiting in the room and I feel a wave of relief I haven't been left till last.

Faye meets me by the door and guides me back into the long hallway she brought me down earlier. As we walk, my mind keeps repeating that word—*talented*. There had been such reverence in the woman's voice when she had uttered it earlier. People here must think being talented is pretty special.

I ask Faye again about finding Sebastian, but she gives me the same answer as the woman from the session. The information is only for immediate family.

'But I'm basically his family,' I protest. 'I lived with him for several years in the ARC. Can't you just check where he is on your tablet?'

Faye hesitates before shaking her head. 'I'm sorry Elle, I can't give you that information,' she responds again.

I stop walking. 'Please. I have no one else up here...'

She pauses a few steps ahead of me and slowly turns. 'When was he taken?' she asks, reluctantly.

'About two weeks ago.'

She smiles slightly and nods at me. 'If it was that recently then it's very likely he will be at your school, here in East Hope. I'm sure you'll find him there. Now, shall we go?'

I want to believe her, as we continue to walk down the hallway, but something about her inability to meet my eyes makes me less certain she's being totally honest with me.

When we finally exit the building my spirits soar. The sunshine makes me want to jump around with excitement or do a crazy happy dance. I still can't quite believe the feel of its warm caress. I look down at my skin and the light blonde hairs on my arm almost glow under it.

Faye watches me curiously. I must look like such an idiot staring at my arm hair with such interest. She tries to hide a smile. 'You'll have to be careful for the first few months up here. It will take a while for your skin to get used to the UV radiation from the sun. If you're in it for too long you'll be at risk of getting sunburnt,' she says.

I look at her questioningly. 'Sunburnt?'

'I forget with some of you younger kids, how little you remember. Just take my word for it. If you stay in the sun too long your skin will burn red, and you'll be in a lot of pain for a few days.'

I vaguely remember hearing something about that before. I look down at my pale arm again though and find it hard to believe it could burn red just from being outside.

She turns round a corner and leads me down a narrow alleyway. The sunshine disappears behind me and the cool shadow of the building covers us as I follow. In this narrow space, I feel like I'm enveloped in concrete. I look around for at least some hint of nature, and only spot a small dejected looking tree.

'Come on, let's get you in the car,' she says. We veer off the alley to a big concrete square filled with cars.

'Do we just pick one?' I ask. She muffles a laugh and pulls out a key. She presses the button on it and the lights flash on one of the cars several times.

'No, that's our car there,' she explains, as we walk towards a weather-beaten black car. It has the same sleek and streamlined body of the cars in that video game the boys always play, 'Speed Junkie IV.' It shows hints of its age though, with patches of rust on the edges of the car doors.

14

Faye opens a door and motions for me to get in. As I sit, I glide my hands along the rough leather texture of the seat. The interior is worn and tired looking, the shiny wooden dashboard has chips in it and the carpet has seen better days.

The door slams shut next to me and, seconds later, I hear the *pop* of the door on the other side of the car opening. Faye slides into the seat next to me. She fiddles around with the keys and different knobs and buttons, and then looks across at me when the car engine rumbles to life.

'Seatbelt.' She flicks her eyes up to something behind me. I turn and find the contraption. It's similar to the one in the helicopter. After a few seconds of playing with it, and glancing over to watch what Faye does with hers, I manage to figure it out.

The car hums as it's awoken, and music blasts from the speakers immersing us in some foreign tune. The wheels squeal against the concrete as the car accelerates away, the engine roaring as it builds momentum. It moves so fast I feel like my whole body is being forced back into the seat. I grip my hands tightly into its leather edges for comfort.

As the car veers out onto a wide street I feel dumbstruck by the combination of total beauty and awesome terror of my surroundings. The few other cars on the road hurtle past us, their motors choking and humming as they drive. Our own car quickly darts in and out of the long, cool shadows of the skyscrapers that tower over us; the sun flickering across my eyes through the tiny gaps between them.

The buildings all stand in a row that extends out to the horizon as far as the eye can see. The magnificent structures materialise for only a moment in the distance and then, before I know it, they vanish behind us as we pass. It's amazing to see them so close, to truly see the city. And all to the tune of some song I've never heard before.

I feel extremely insignificant. There are so many people, even more than I'd thought from the air. Hundreds of faces wiz past the side window of the car. They move so quickly I'm unable to even hope to catch a glimpse of Sebastian.

I feel a sense of guilt and misplacement as we drive. I don't belong up here, with these people who are supposedly special—special enough to be allowed to walk freely above ground.

Eventually the car slows and pulls over on the side of the road.

'Here we are,' Faye says, as she gets out of the car. I pull uselessly at the seatbelt several times before spotting the massive red 'release' button.

As I step out of the car I am filled with a sense of dread. I'm so consumed by it I don't watch where I step. I stumble as my foot fails to find the sidewalk, instead ending up sodden in a puddle of gutter water. I shake my leg, the bottoms of my wet greys now clinging to it.

'Are you okay?' Faye asks, rushing to help me up.

'I'm fine,' I say, attempting to smile at the situation, but struggling because my wet pants are already forgotten and my dread of living with strangers has returned.

'You will be living in here,' Faye says, pointing to one of the large buildings that tower over us. It's just like the rest of them—a wall of glass shimmering a reflection of the bright and sunny city.

I'm trying hard not to be scared as I cross the road towards the building. Everything was so surreal up until this moment, but now reality is crashing down around me. For a fleeting moment I consider trying to escape, but I know I shouldn't. Nothing bad has happened so far and I have no idea where I'd go, or what I'd do, if I did try to run.

'This way Elle,' Faye calls.

We walk through a set of glass revolving doors and head across to an elevator. I clench my teeth as she presses the button. I'd much prefer to take the stairs. As we get in, Faye hits the button for floor twelve.

'We're setting you up with Cathy and Paul Mason. They have a son, Jackson, who's ten, and a daughter, Beth, who's your age. They've had quite a few newbies over the years, so they're used to the adjustment and will be really good at helping you get on your feet.'

The elevator dings as we reach the twelfth floor. My heart is beating quickly now.

Faye knocks on the door and a man opens it. I hadn't even realised I'd been moving, but I've placed myself directly behind her. I'm huddling myself like a crazed person. *Deep breaths.* I place my arms by my side and step next to Faye.

I look up, into the man's eyes, and he's not at all what I expected. He's tall and dressed in a smart brown suit. His dark hair is combed back neatly and his eyes are serious, but not unfriendly. He's looking at me kindly, like he's actually happy I'm here.

The door opens wider and a woman comes to stand next to him. She's short, almost comically so next to him, and slightly dumpy. Her smile is warm and I get the feeling she wants to wrap me up in a massive hug. I want to relax at the sight, because they both look like good people, but my body holds stiff.

My nose catches a whiff of something from inside the apartment. It's rich and fragrant. My mouth begins to water as I try to imagine what it could be. I haven't eaten yet today and, for the first time in this exceedingly long day, I notice how famished I am.

'Hi Cathy, Paul. I'm Faye from the reintegration centre. I commed you earlier about Elle...'

'Yes, of course. Won't you both come in?' the woman responds. Faye enters the apartment first and I cautiously follow.

The woman, Cathy, takes both my hands in hers. 'Elle, it's so nice to meet you,' she says. She's just trying to be nice, I remind myself, as she continues holding my hands, refusing to let go.

'Well, aren't you lovely,' she gushes. She's half a head shorter than me and has to lean her head back as she gazes up at my face.

When she finally drops my hands from hers, the man gently pats me on the back. 'I'm Paul and this is my wife Cathy. The kids are at school, but they should be home shortly. We're really looking forward to having you here and want you to feel like this is your home.'

I nod up at him, completely lost for what to say.

'You both know the drill,' Faye interrupts. 'Elle, if there's

anything ... you have my username and can comm me at any time. Good luck. I'll check up on you in a couple of weeks to see how you're doing.'

She is leaving already? I peer at the Masons, who stand there with their welcoming smiles plastered across their faces. They seem nice, but I'm not ready to be left with these strangers.

Faye stands at the door waiting for me to acknowledge her departure.

'Thanks,' I say to her, attempting to sound more confident than I feel.

'It's no problem.' She gives a little wave goodbye and starts walking towards the elevator.

'I need to head back to the office,' Paul says, bending down to pick up a briefcase. 'I'll see you both at dinner and we can have a proper chat. Get to know each other a little better.' He jogs down the hallway to catch up with Faye.

Cathy closes the door behind him and I stand inside the entrance, my arms folded across my chest as I blankly stare her down. I'm waiting for the smiles to go and the act to drop. These people can't be this nice.

'Here, I'll show you around...' Cathy beckons me forward.

I frown for a brief second, before dropping my arms and following.

Silently, I shadow her as she flits around the apartment. Cathy obviously takes great pride in her home. She is highly excitable and revels in showing me all of its massive rooms.

Like all the other buildings I've seen this morning, the entire place has floor-to-ceiling windows and when we enter the lounge room I'm drawn to them as soon as I notice the warm light flooding inside.

I carefully approach the glass. There's a massive drop down the sheer surface of the window to the ground, where the people and cars are all in miniature. I expect to be unnerved by the sight, but the feeling of being up so high thrills me. There is so much to see out

there and the world beyond the glass is huge. It's so open and free, and though my stomach drops as I look down, my chest feels like it opens up to embrace the wide world in front of me.

The view out over the city is simply breathtaking. Buildings high and low sprawl across the city before me, their windows shimmering golden under the sun's heat. There is no sign of the barren snow-covered wasteland that stretches from the surface above the ARC all the way to the edge of the city.

I can't believe I've spent my life without this incredible view. Cathy calls me away from the window to continue, 'the tour,' as she puts it. The next room on the tour is apparently mine, and Cathy can't stop smiling as she goes for the big reveal.

It's huge. Unbelievably huge. Although I guess that's to be expected in an apartment so enormous.

I step into the room and look around it, taking it all in. It's beautiful. A double bed sits in the centre covered in sheets that are a pastel pink floral print. It looks so enticing I feel the urge to run over and jump on it.

There's an old ornate wooden wardrobe against one wall and a gorgeous embellished mirror against the other. At the end of the room the floor-to-ceiling windows continue, framed by thick curtains. Everything in here is beautiful, but like the rest of the apartment they appear timeworn, maybe salvaged from the world before impact? The room is larger and far prettier than the standard white quarters I shared with Quinn in the ARC, but without her presence it feels remarkably empty.

'Elle?' Cathy asks, from where she stands in the doorway.

'Mmm?' I turn to face her.

'I've been baking in the kitchen. You must be starved. Would you like to come with me and have something to eat?'

'Sure.' My stomach grumbles in agreement, my ravenous hunger now provoked. I follow her through to a bright, open kitchen that's all white marble benches and cool steel appliances. It looks like serious cooking must happen in here. It's almost the same size as the kitchens in the ARC, and they cook for hundreds of people.

She bends down with a towel in hand and takes a tray out of the oven, placing it on the cooktop. I then realise what the smell was ... cookies!

'Have they told you much about what's happened to you and how everything works around here?' she asks, as she begins transferring the cookies onto a plate.

'Sort of, but it felt like there were things they left out.'

She sighs, sounding disappointed. 'I guess that's almost to be expected. They're always so busy processing people; they're never too good at explaining everything to our new arrivals. More often than not I have people arrive here with absolutely no idea what's going on. It can be very scary. How're you feeling?'

'Okay,' I lie. Well, it's not exactly a lie. She raises one eyebrow, giving me a knowing look.

'I've been better,' I admit.

'I can imagine.' She places the plate of cookies in front of me. 'Careful, they're still hot.'

I pick one up and blow on the corner of it before taking a small bite and groaning in delight.

'Good?'

'Mmm, so good.'

'Should we take them to the living room? We can sit there and have a chat if you like?' I nod and pick up the plate to follow her through.

Sitting on the couch I have a perfect view of the city outside. I bet I'll even be able to see the sunset from here.

'For the moment we'll give you some of Beth's clothing to wear, but tomorrow I'm thinking we'll go to the refuse centre and get you some clothes of your own. There's never anything too fancy there, mostly clothing from before impact, but at least you won't be in those greys anymore. You must be so sick of them.' I nod in agreement as I bite down on another cookie. It's never bothered me before, not when there's been no other choice, but the thought of wearing something different every day is exciting.

'Can't I go to school tomorrow?' I ask. The chance to maybe see Sebastian at school in the morning is too hard to resist.

'Maybe in a few days,' she responds. 'We want you to get settled in first.'

'I'm fine, *really*,' I emphasise.

'How about we see how you feel after tomorrow?'

'Okay.' I feel slightly defeated, but one more day should be fine. I'll make certain Cathy lets me go the following day.

'You've been enrolled in East Hope High. It's where our eldest, Beth, goes. I think you'll find the subjects are similar to the ones you did in the ARC, so you should be back in routine fairly quickly. The only subject that can be quite a challenge are the special studies sessions—'

'What are those?' I ask, interrupting her.

'It's essentially a class to help you develop your talent.'

I swallow uncomfortably. There had been no mention of special classes focused on our talents during reintegration. What if I'm found out?

'How much were you told in your reintegration session?' Cathy asks me carefully, when she notes the worry on my face.

'We learnt about the talents, but nothing about special training sessions...'

'Oh,' she looks at me, confused, 'I thought they would have mentioned it. Special studies is the most important lesson at school if you want to be recruited, which of course, you do.'

The front door clicks behind me and there's movement as people walk through it. The front door slams shut and a girl's voice calls out 'Mum? We're home!'

The sound of the voice makes me nervous. Beth, I think her name was. I'd been relieved to know I'd be living with someone my own age, but I still feel a little anxious about meeting her. I wish she hadn't arrived here so soon; there are so many questions I still want to ask Cathy.

'Mum?' The girl enters the room from behind me.

Cathy looks up to her, a warm smile across her face. 'Hi Honey. We have someone new staying with us. This is Elle,' she says, introducing me.

I swivel myself around on the couch to greet Beth. But when I turn and stare this girl in the eyes I know immediately Beth isn't her name. It's April.

What the hell is Sebastian's sister doing here?

CHAPTER THREE

'Hi Elle, I'm *Beth*,' April says, strongly emphasising the name I know can't be true. There's a warning glint in her eyes as she looks at me, causing all the excitement I'd just felt at seeing her after so many years apart to falter. Why is she pretending to be someone else?

I look at April up and down. She's dressed in a charcoal grey dress with black stockings and a black cardigan. Her eye makeup is black and despite being up here on the surface, she still retains a pale pallor to her skin. Her hair is several shades darker than I remember, but there's no changing her blue eyes. They are just the same as Sebastian's. My stomach clenches as I look into them, she reminds me so much of her brother. What on earth is she doing here?

'Uh ... hi ... Beth?' I'm at a loss for words. I clench my hands into fists on my lap and try to stop them from shaking. This is all too much.

A young boy bolts into the room, his arms out wide as he swoops and circles like he's a plane. This must be Jackson. He looks like he's had too much sugar the way he's practically bouncing off walls.

When he sees me he stops, freezing to the spot. He gapes at me, then over at Cathy, before running back out of the room.

'He's not too good with new people,' Cathy explains. 'But he'll come around.'

'Elle was it?' April says. 'I'm heading down to the local courts to play some basketball. Do you want to come?'

It takes me a moment to respond, as I have no idea how to act around her. She's treating me like I'm a complete stranger, but I can tell by the way she looks at me, she knows exactly who I am.

'Yeah, that'd be great,' I say. Maybe if I'm alone with her I'll be able to get some answers about why she's acting so differently?

'I've got some clothes and shoes you can borrow if you like?'

'Okay.' I stand and go to follow her, but quickly turn to Cathy. I still have so many unanswered questions.

'Go ahead,' she says, standing herself and gathering the empty cookie plate. 'It will be good for you to meet some of the other kids before you start school. We'll see you at dinner.'

I follow Beth into her room. It's next door to mine and similar in that it looks out over the city, but this is where the similarity ends. There are no pink flowered quilt covers in here. Instead, the walls are painted a dark, gloomy grey colour and the bed is covered with black sheets. With Beth's own sombre attire, she's almost lost in the wallpaper in here.

She takes some exercise gear out of the drawers and throws it to me.

'April, is it really you?' It's difficult to keep the happiness from my voice and takes every ounce of my self-control not to run up to her and give her a hug.

'Don't call me that,' she spits through her teeth. She slams the drawer shut, the small dresser rocking from the impact.

'Okay ... sorry.' I hadn't expected such a venomous reaction.

'What are you doing here?' she whispers, her eyes flicking over to the open door.

'I was about to ask *you* the same thing,' I reply, in an equally hushed tone of voice.

'*I* live here,' she responds. This isn't the April who was once my best friend. She's changed so much in the last few years. If it wasn't for her deep blue eyes I can't imagine I would have even recognised her.

'So...' she urges.

'I was taken,' I respond. 'Then they brought me here. I was so relieved when I saw you just now. What's gotten into you? Why are they calling you Beth?'

My ears perk up and we both look to the open door as we hear the patter of small footsteps in the hallway.

Beth looks back to me, but the anger from her face slides and she sighs. 'Get changed. We'll talk outside.'

WALKING through the streets of Hope I am truly able to appreciate how vast the city is. It's exactly how I always imagined a city above the ground would've looked before impact, and it's amazing.

There are the buildings, which of course I'd seen from the car, but they aren't just the faceless walls of glass I'd seen from a distance. Up close there's so much more to them. Many of the windows hold these colourful and old, weathered signs, advertising shops from before impact, like a poignant reminder of the world we lost. Several of the shops have been restored and are filled with all types of goods up for trade.

I pass an enormous cafeteria, teeming with people, with wide open doors that allow tables and chairs to spill out onto the sidewalk. There's a grocery store that displays fruit and vegetables for sale in massive crates out front, and a large barrel of flowers by the doorway. The flowers are arranged in brilliantly vivid bunches and the colours and fragrance from them is almost too marvellous to be believed.

It's far louder than I ever could have imagined and the noise is constant and ceaseless. Away from the Atrium or the dining hall in the ARC there was only ever the soft hum of the lights. Here there's never a second of peace. There's the sound of car engines purring, music, odd beeping noises, people walking and talking, the sound of some machine drilling in the distance. And those are just the noises I can label.

I find my eyes are drawn to anything and everything. Seeing people wearing different and strange clothes, the blue sky, the sun, trees, buildings, cars, and bicycles. Looking at them all I can't decide what astounds me the most.

I re-adjust the clothes Beth gave me. I'm wearing long, black bootleg track pants, a plain white t-shirt and a black zip up jacket. The material feels so strange and foreign against my skin. I never thought I'd miss my greys, but I feel strangely exposed without them.

A burst of laughter erupts from up ahead as a boy unsteadily rides a bike down the street with a girl sitting on the handlebars. They both squeal and laugh as the bike begins to tip over.

Beth walks next to me, not nearly as overwhelmed by the world outside as I am. I glance down at my fidgeting hands as I work up the courage to ask her the question I've been desperate to ask since the moment I saw her.

'Do you know where Sebastian is?' I ask.

'What do you mean?' she responds.

'He was taken. I need to find him.'

'What?' She stops me mid-step, grabbing my arm. 'He's here?'

'You didn't know?'

'Clearly.' She takes a breath and clears her throat. 'What about my dad? How is he?' She may sound nonchalant, but her eyes show the depth of her anxiety. She must've been desperate to ask me about her family.

'He's okay. He's not handling Sebastian being taken too well though.'

'When did Sebastian get taken?'

'A couple of weeks ago. How is it you don't know? They said he'd be at school.'

She drops her hand from my arm and her cool façade returns. 'I don't know if you've noticed, but Hope's a big place and East Hope High isn't the only school. He's not there.'

My shoulders slouch, defeated. 'I don't understand. They said he'd be there. You don't know where he is then?'

'Obviously.'

'What can we do? Could we try a search for his username on our cuffs?' I ask.

She shakes her head. 'Can't search for users on these. You can only get them by bumping cuffs.' I search her face closely. I almost believe she doesn't care. *Almost...*

She starts walking again and I have to jog a few steps to catch up with her. We walk in silence for a block, before I attempt to talk to her again.

'I'm so confused ... Beth. Can you please just explain what's going on?'

She doesn't respond.

'Where would they have taken Sebastian? Why are you living with these strangers? Where's your mum?'

'She's at home. Probably starting dinner about now.'

'I know where Cathy is. I mean your *real* mum.'

She ignores me and keeps walking.

'They keep talking about people being talented. I still can't even begin to wrap my head around that one. Could you at least tell me about that?' I let my irritation seep into my voice.

Beth laughs heartlessly under her breath again, but keeps walking.

'C'mon. Please?' She continues to ignore me so I reach out and grab her arm, stopping her. 'Would you please tell me?'

She looks me up and down. A malicious smirk turns at the corner of her lips. 'Oh, I can do better than tell you...' she murmurs.

She looks around before turning down an alleyway. Nervously I follow. It's narrow, and evening has started to hit, so thick shadows are sprawled across the walls and at my feet. The hustle and bustle of the city disappears as we move away from the street. The eerie quiet sends a shiver down my spine. I guess not everything above ground is all sunshine.

'Where are you taking me?' I call, as I trudge after her. Again, she doesn't turn around. The smell of something rancid reaches my nose as I near a dumpster that is overflowing with its filth. I scrunch up my face in disgust and begin to breath through my mouth, sticking as close to the opposite wall of the alley as possible, while I walk past it.

'C'mon Beth—Shit!' I curse as I stumble over an empty crate. I bend down to roll up the bottom of the pants Beth has lent me. This is ridiculous. Where is she taking me? She's not acting like herself.

When I look up Beth is nowhere to be seen.

'Beth?' I slowly straighten up. The other end of the alley is too far for Beth to have reached in such a short time, and there is nothing between the exit and me. She's completely disappeared.

I pull my jacket in closer and, tucking my arms around me, I half-turn to check over my shoulder. I'm still quite close to where I entered the alley.

I look back to where I'd last seen Beth. Maybe I should head back to the apartment? I have no idea where she's gone.

My eyebrows crease as I try to decide what to do next. I'm not certain I'll be able to find my way back. The buildings had all looked so similar and I'd been so distracted on our walk here, I hadn't seen any landmarks that could help me find my way back. I look down at my CommuCuff, uncertain how well it would be able to direct me out here.

Maybe Beth just got a little more ahead of me than I thought? I take a few hesitant steps forward. 'Beth?' I call louder this time, hoping she can hear me.

'Behind you,' Beth's voice whispers in my ear. I leap up and squeal with surprise, as my heart jumps into my mouth. I hold my throat with my hand and bend over, trying to calm myself.

'Where did you come from?' I wheeze. She pats me on the back and continues down the alley.

'Told you I'd show you what being *talented* was,' she taunts.

'What are you talking about? You didn't show me anything.'

'Come on Elle, think about it.' She turns back and taps her finger against her head. I can tell she's enjoying this. I look around for where she'd been hiding.

'Seriously where'd you go?' She shrugs in response. I want to glare at her, or say something spiteful, but I'm distracted. Something's different about her eyes. It's like the rings are brighter than usual. They're almost purple in colour, rather than her normal blue.

'What's wrong with your eyes?' I ask.

'Nothing!' She lifts her hands to rub them and turns to keep walking. I start to follow, but then stop. I don't want to play this game anymore.

'April, what is going on?' She stops in her tracks when she hears her name, turns, and marches back towards me.

'Elle, you really can't call me that.' The sarcasm has dropped and instead her voice has a pleading edge to it.

'Then you really need to explain...'

'Fine.' She pushes her hands through her hair. 'What do you want to know?'

'Tell me more about being talented,' I ask quietly, scared to say something that will raise her hackles again.

She huffs out an irritated breath before she begins. 'People who are tainted have developed talents, but it's not something that will affect you too much. You've ended up in East Hope. Everyone knows you only go to East Hope if you're an untalent.'

'A what?'

'An untalent,' she groans as though I'm completely thick. 'It's a person who's been affected by the mutation, but doesn't develop any new faculties that allow them to do the extraordinary. Most people are untalents. Often they have some capacity for precognition or retrocognition. Untalented precogs barely even count as talents in my book.'

Utter confusion must be written all over my face. It's like she's speaking a completely different language. She catches my expression and rolls her eyes. 'Weren't you listening in your reintegration session?'

I stare at her blankly. 'They didn't explain in this kind of detail...'

'It's simple. Untalents have very weak talents. A talented person might have a mutation that enables them to move large objects with just their mind. But, an untalent with a similar mutation might only be able to lift a pen a few inches off the ground.'

'And you?'

'I'm in the east, so what do you think?'

I look at her uncertainly. 'I think you just disappeared from far in front of me and then somehow reappeared behind me.'

She laughs hysterically. 'Elle, I was hiding behind the dumpster over there.' I turn around to look in the direction she's pointing and see the dumpster I'd walked past earlier.

I fold my arms across my chest and avoid meeting her eyes when I turn back. 'Oh,' I reply. I shouldn't have said what I thought, but she disappeared from sight. With everything that's going on, what did she expect me to think? I'm not even certain I believe her dumpster explanation. I would've seen her. I shiver and rub my arms. The alley is starting to get quite cold now and I'm not used to such an unregulated temperature.

'There are, of course, some people in Hope who could probably do something like that,' she continues. 'I doubt we've really even begun to see the extent of what humans are now capable of.'

'What about the people you live with, your family?'

'Untalents.'

'Okay. So where are the people that can disappear?'

'They're in the north. On the other side of the river.' She walks towards the wall lining the alley and sits on a crate. 'But untalents aren't allowed to go there. It's too...' her voice trails off as she looks for the word, 'dangerous, not to mention illegal.'

'What do you mean by dangerous?'

'Just trust me. Even if you could go there, you wouldn't want to.

Besides, what could be worse than going to a place and being surrounded by people who can do things you can only dream of?'

If only she knew how close her last sentence hits home for me. I want to tell her the truth about me, but she's acting so strangely and completely different to the girl I was once so close to in the ARC. I'm not certain if I can trust her now

'Where do you think Sebastian is?' I ask.

She shrugs like she doesn't care. 'He could be anywhere.'

'I don't understand why they didn't put him with you. They said the only reason I'm fostered out is because I don't have family here.'

'I... I don't...' She stands up. 'Listen, I think I've answered enough of your questions. We should head back before Mum gets worried.' She stalks off down the alley without another word.

'But she's not your mum...' I say, under my breath, before jogging to catch up with her.

CHAPTER FOUR

I stare out over the city from my rooftop vantage point. The sun is high overhead and the light sparkles as it dances across the city below me. Cathy hasn't let me leave the building since we went to the refuse centre this morning, so I'm grateful I've at least found a place in this complex where I can be outside.

It was exciting going to the refuse centre, where most people in the east go to get their clothes. Set in this big, ancient looking warehouse, it was huge compared to the handful of clothing boutiques I'd walked past yesterday, where only the highly successful have enough credits to shop.

The place was filled with racks of clothing that extended as far as the eye could see. The clothes weren't nearly as fancy as the dresses I used to borrow from the costume room in the ARC but, like the ARC, everything there had been previously worn.

I found myself nervous yet eager as we picked through the clothes racks. I'd never had the freedom to pick what clothes I would like to wear each day and it was overwhelming trying to decide what to get. I still can't believe I'll never have to wear my greys again.

I lean my arms down on the outer ledge of the building and peer over the edge. It's such a long way down from up here, but I have no problem with the height. The surrounding structures, which looked so tall from the ground, are like children next to the Mason's towering apartment building.

I can easily see over the neighbouring rooftops and off to the horizon. From up here you can even make out the snow and ice that still grips the far edge of the city. My eyes drop quickly from the sight. I don't want to think about the impact winter anymore.

I turn away from the view to look back across the rooftop. There's a small garden up here that is completely wild, with plants that have taken over the fenced off area. There are strange leafy bushes that stick out at all angles, and weeds growing throughout the planter beds. Then, there are these incredible soft pink roses, that tumble and cascade over the ground and up around an archway that marks the entrance to the space. It's beautiful despite its untamed growth, or maybe because of it. Gemma would love it up here. She broke into the plantation in the ARC about as many times as I did.

I lean my head back to the sky and relish the feeling of the sun's rays against my skin. It almost tingles across it. If I was forced underground for another fifteen years, I'm certain I'd never again forget the amazing feeling of it cocooning my body in its warmth.

As I lower my head and turn to look back at the view of the city, a wave of homesickness hits me. The surface is amazing, but I miss the gentle, droning hum of the ARC. The comfort that comes with knowing there's a schedule, that every day follows the same routine. I miss the safety and security of knowing the people around me.

Most of all I miss Quinn. Is it really only a day since I saw her face? I shake my head trying to clear the thoughts of Quinn from my mind. I'll completely lose it if I think about her.

When I turn back to look at the view, I feel slightly overwhelmed by the enormity of the city. There are so many buildings, with so many people. *Where are you Sebastian?*

I don't even know where to begin to look and I doubt Cathy and Paul will be able to help me. I asked Paul last night how I could find my friend, hoping he could provide some insight since he works for the government, but he said there was nothing he could do. April almost fell off her seat, choking on her mouthful of chicken, when I'd brought that subject up at dinner.

Sorry, not April, Beth. She's changed so much since being taken. The young girl I had known in the ARC had been an adventurous, fun, free-spirited person. This 'Beth' is so distant I worry the April I knew is gone.

I just wish I could understand what she's been through, what happened to change her so drastically. She hasn't talked to me since our walk though and appears to be avoiding me.

'What are you doing up here?' Speak of the devil. It's hard to mistake Beth's voice from behind me. I'd been so caught up in my musings I hadn't even heard the elevator ding on her arrival. I continue looking out over the city as she comes to stand next to me.

'Just getting some air and enjoying the view. How about you, April?' I ask, already feeling apprehensive about her response. I don't want to fight with her and, from the sound of her bristling tone of voice, she's raring for a confrontation.

'Beth.' She corrects me angrily. I turn to her and can almost see the tension rolling off her shoulders.

'Sorry. I keep forgetting.' I sigh and look back at the view. 'Have you had any thoughts about where Sebastian could be? How we could try to find him?'

'No,' she responds. She doesn't sound like she's given it a moment's thought, but I find that hard to believe.

'I was thinking about going back to the reintegration centre to see if they had any information on him. Do you think they'd help me?'

Beth laughs. 'Yeah, I'm sure they'd love to help you. Gosh, why hadn't I thought of that?'

I take a step back from the ledge and frown at her. 'Why wouldn't they want to help?'

'They won't even let you through the front doors of the reintegration centre, let alone give you information on someone.'

'Why not?'

Beth shrugs. 'I don't even want to help you, and he's my brother. Why would they?'

'You don't mean that.'

'Don't I?'

'Seriously April, what's happened to you? We were once best friends and I can't understand why you won't talk to me. Why you want nothing to do with me, why you don't want to find your brother. What's happened to change you so much?'

'You wouldn't understand. And it's Beth,' she says, her voice dropping low.

I wait for her to continue, hoping she will open up, but she doesn't say a word.

'If you ever want to talk ... I'm here,' I tell her.

She opens her mouth, but then shuts it tightly and turns away. I sadly turn away myself and walk towards the elevator. I shove the down button hard when I reach it and the doors slide open. I enter and turn to press the button for our floor, but my fingers hover over it for a moment before I push. Beth stands at the edge of the building, facing away from me with her shoulders slouched forward and her dark hair draped over her face. She looks so alone.

The lift doors close and I rub my fingers in a gentle circle around my temples. I'd always hoped I'd one day see April again, but I can't bear to see her this way. She seems so lost and I hate she won't let me in to help her—even if there was nothing I could do, I just want her to know she has someone she can talk to.

When the doors open at level 12, my feet don't move. Instead, I hit the ground floor button. I can't face another second in that apartment right now. I don't care what Cathy said about staying in the building, I didn't go through hell to get out of the ARC and find Sebastian only to be imprisoned in an apartment on the surface.

I walk out through the big glass doors in the foyer and let my feet guide me away from the apartment building in the direction of the reintegration centre. Well, where I think it is, seeing as I don't have

the address keyed into my cuff. April is wrong about them not wanting to help. She has to be.

After twenty minutes of walking past identical buildings my resolve begins to waver. The buildings extend tirelessly into the distance and the reintegration centre is nowhere in sight. It hadn't taken long to travel between there and the Macon's by car yesterday, but walking is taking ages.

I stop walking and step into one of the building's doorways. I can't even be certain I'm going in the right direction to get to the reintegration centre so instead I comm Faye. Maybe I can convince her to let me know where he is? She said I could comm her about anything, so I'm sure she won't mind.

'Hello,' she answers, after one ring.

'Hi Faye, this is Elle Winters. We met yesterday for reintegration—'

'Is everything okay?' she interrupts.

'Yes, everything's fine.'

'Then why are you comming me?'

'It's about the friend I mentioned yesterday. I'm still trying to find him and he's not at my school. Can you please tell me how to get in touch with him?'

'I'm sorry Elle, as I already told you, I can only give that information to immediate family. If your friend is not in East Hope then there's nothing I can do.'

'But—'

'Please only comm me if you have a *real* problem.' It takes me a second to realise she's already disconnected the comm, and another moment to grasp the fact that it wasn't an accident.

I slowly lower my arm down to my side and move back onto the sidewalk. She didn't even consider helping me with Sebastian? Can the rules on giving out that information really be so strict?

April would be able to get the details, but she's pretending to be someone else and has already refused to help me find Sebastian.

I continue walking down the road, strolling slower now as I feel my sense of purpose weaken. I can't understand why it's such a big deal. Would I get the same frosty reception if I went to the reintegration centre? I want to believe they'd help me, but if my assigned contact person there won't help, why would anyone else?

I consider returning to the Mason's, but a part of me still hopes I'll find the reintegration centre, so I continue slowly walking down the road.

More people spill out onto the sidewalk as I continue, and I try to ignore my building anxiety at being surrounded by a mass of strangers. In the ARC you would usually have at least some faint recognition of people you passed in the hallways, or the Atrium. It was rare you didn't recognise them at all.

I search every face I pass for Sebastian. It's probably a lost cause, hoping I'll simply bump into him on the street, but I'm not sure what else to try. Every time I look at a face, and it's not him, I lose a small ounce of hope I'll ever find him again.

I try not to stare too much at the people I pass, but I find it hard to stop myself when I notice a woman walking towards me with a dress that changes colour as she moves. As the skirt gently ripples in the wind, the colours shift from the lightest hint of pink to a deep rich emerald green colour, and then on to a startling, brilliant hue of blue.

What I would do for an outfit like that! My jeans and sweater, which were so exciting when I'd picked them this morning, now feel nearly as dull as my greys. I focus in on the morphing colours and try to figure out how the dress can change the way it does. The woman notices me and the dress abruptly shifts to a plain white colour. I drop my eyes and focus intently on the concrete ground. I must look like such an idiot, staring at her with my eyes wide and mouth hanging open.

Once I pass the woman, I look back over my shoulder at her and the dress changes colour again. It dawns on me the dress couldn't possibly change colours in that way and the woman must be doing it; her talent must somehow be allowing her to change the colour of the material.

I shake my head with disbelief. I've finally seen one in real life. I'd expected my first interaction with a talent to be something spectacular or, at the very least, useful. Maybe she could use her talent as some form of camouflage?

The way the Masons go on about them, I thought I'd be interacting with Gods. They'd been all the news had broadcasted about last night, and there was even this show that aired after called, 'Talented'. Apparently Paul and Cathy watch it religiously. They act like having a high-level talent is the best thing that could possibly happen to you.

I'm not so sure. I want to know more about it all before I make up my mind. Maybe I just have to get used to the idea?

On Talented, they featured a man who was unbelievably strong. He could lift a car up over his head without even breaking a sweat. Then, there was this little boy who could remember everything he'd ever read. He stood there and recited the exact wording from any page of any book that was thrown at him. He was barely old enough to read, let alone have the ability to recount page 26 of 'Lord of the Flies'.

I guess it would be cool to be able to do that sort of thing, but it's not something I have to worry about anytime soon. If anything, I have to focus on not appearing completely normal.

When I turn back to watch where I'm walking I notice trees up ahead. As I get closer it's clear the greenery extends far into the distance and I'm looking at a park. My pace quickens as I hurry to get to it. It's so lush and alive compared to the rigid glass towers I associate with the surface.

I step onto the road to cross over to it, excitement urging me onwards. A bell rings out a small chime in the distance. Ding, ding. The entrance to the park is a dirt pathway that disappears into the thick foliage. The chiming of the bell dings louder and more urgently. I turn to the sound and a bike is hurtling straight for me. I squeal and jump back onto the curb.

'Idiot!' the man yells, as he whooshes past. I hold my hand to my throat, breathless. I *am* such an idiot. I nearly got run down. Cathy warned me about checking before crossing the road. I'd been excited about the park though and hadn't thought.

Once I catch my breath I make my way across the road again, this time checking very carefully in each direction before crossing. I wander onto the pathway and follow it into the beautiful greenery.

I can't have been close to finding the reintegration centre, I would've remembered passing a place like this yesterday.

The pathway is lined with trees and it's cool under the canopy created by the branches that fan overhead. Light flickers through the leaves, creating a mosaic of shadows across the hard dirt I walk on. I breathe in and relish the taste of the fresh, crisp air. This is exactly what I imagined the surface would've been like before impact. I never dared to imagine it could be like this in my lifetime.

There's an outburst of laughter and yelling in the distance. I look up and out over the grass field that lies ahead. There are people laying out on grassy knolls soaking in the sunshine and beyond them a group of boys playing with a football. They look like they're about my age and when I get closer I stop and watch them curiously. They're standing in a circle bouncing the ball around, trying to make sure it doesn't touch the ground.

They yell and laugh and shove each other around playfully whenever someone drops the ball. The sight makes me miss my friends so much. It will be strange starting school again tomorrow and not knowing anyone. Anyone besides Beth, that is, whom I probably can't count on to show me around.

I shouldn't even be going to school. It feels like a waste of time when April has already told me Sebastian won't be there. I don't have much choice though if I don't want to draw attention to myself.

The boys lose control of the ball they are playing with and it rolls towards me, stopping right in front of my feet. I bend down and pick it up. As I stand there one of the boys from the group runs over to get it. He has ruffled dark blonde hair that sits just above his blue eyes.

As he nears he grins at me. It's one of those contagious smiles, and I can feel myself smiling in response.

'Hey,' he says, when he gets close.

'Hi,' I say, my voice breaks and I quickly clear my throat. This is the first stranger I've talked to in Hope and the first boy my age I've ever met who I haven't known since I was five. He tilts his head slightly as he looks at me.

'Oh, your ball.' I laugh awkwardly as I throw it to him and he catches it easily.

'Thanks.' He looks at me for a moment longer.

'No problem,' I reply. Why is he still looking at me that way?

One of the boys from the game calls him back over.

'See you around,' he says, before running back to his friends. I stand watching them for a moment then quickly move on, as I'm staring—and that's totally creepy.

The cover of leaves overhead begins to thin out and I reach a railing that acts as a barrier to a lake that lies on the other side of it. I stand for a while, leaning on the rusty wrought iron rail looking at the surface, which is dark and reflective in the afternoon light.

As I watch the water slowly meander along I notice it's not a lake, but the river Beth was talking about. Realising this, the tall buildings that line the other side of it become more intriguing. North Hope, I remember, where all the talents live.

There's a bridge that crosses to the other side of the river a little further down. What would happen if I walked across it? I know untalents aren't allowed on the northern side of the river, but I feel curious about it. How strict are they about enforcing the rule?

Lights on the other bank begin to turn on and twinkle, and the sky beyond the bridge becomes an array of burnt orange and deep purple streaks. It's a beautiful sunset; the colours splashed across the horizon are so strong and unique. When the colours fade and the sky turns to a deep blue I turn to head back. The coolness of evening has begun to descend and I feel grateful I'm wearing a sweater, even if it is a loose weave.

I make my way back along the pathway under the dense shelter of trees, where it's already become quite dark. My pace quickens as I begin to worry. I stayed at the river too long. It was so peaceful watching the water flow by me, and I couldn't tear myself away from the sunset. I hadn't thought about nightfall and didn't realise how quickly it would get dark.

My unease only increases as I continue through the park. I haven't seen anyone in a while and the long shadows are becoming darker by the second. I *really* don't want to be left alone out here.

The path I follow reaches a junction and splits off several different ways. I pause as I attempt to remember the path I'd been on earlier. I take a hold of my necklace and twist the chain nervously as I look at the different routes. I'd been distracted by my thoughts earlier and can't exactly remember the pathway home. They'd all twisted and turned so much, meeting up in points before separating again.

Instead of wasting time trying to remember my original route, I pull the directions to the Mason's address up on my CommuCuff. Thankfully Cathy had thought to key them in this morning.

The sky has darkened to a deep navy blue by the time I find my way back to the street. The park behind me is now heavily cloaked in darkness and the lamps that line the street form a welcome beacon. They're bright but I still don't feel particularly safe.

There are so many strangers hurrying around at the moment. In lessons back in the ARC, we'd learnt how risky walking the city at night could be and how safe the ARC was in comparison. I half expect to be robbed.

Do people still do that?

I hug my arms against my chest and keep my head down as I walk. I avoid eye contact with everyone and make my way home as quickly as possible. As I get closer to the Mason's I recognise a few of the buildings I pass and begin to feel more at ease.

As I stare up at one building that towers above and the bright lights that emanate from within I accidently clip a man. 'Sorry!' I

turn to apologise. My heart stops as I look at the back of his head. I swear I know *that* head.

'Ryan?' I say. The man keeps walking, slowly disappearing in the crowd. 'Ryan!' I call. I duck and weave between people, running up to get to him. Could it really be him?

I grab his arm, causing him to swing around. As the man turns I jump back in shock. I've grabbed a man who definitely isn't Ryan.

'Sorry!' I exclaim as he looks at me, surprised. 'I thought you were ... well, never mind.'

I don't wait for his response. Instead, I run back in the direction I was heading, my cheeks flaming red with embarrassment. I'm officially losing my mind.

CHAPTER FIVE

It's hard to force my eyes awake in the morning. I feel so cosy curled up in bed. I just want to stay here all day. I bolt upright as my brain switches on and I remember, *today's my first day at school*. I groan and almost settle back under my covers. I don't want to go.

I look over at the clock. It's 8:15 A.M. *Shit!* I jump out of bed. Beth had warned me, in no uncertain terms, she left for school at eight and if I wasn't ready she'd quite happily leave without me.

I run to Beth's room and knock urgently on the door.

'Beth?' I call out. There's no response. I open the door a crack and poke my head in. She's not there.

'Damn it!'

I dash into the bathroom to brush my teeth and wash my face before running back to my room to throw on the clothes I'd set aside for today. I swoop my hair back into a ponytail, pick up the bag Cathy had packed for me and swing it over my shoulder.

There's no time for breakfast, so I grab an apple and walk towards the front door. I stop still as my hand curls around the door handle. I don't know where the school is, and Cathy has already left to take Jackson to his primary school.

I step back from the door and pace back and forth as I try to remember what Cathy had said about getting to school. She hadn't gone into too much detail though, as Beth was supposed to take me there. She didn't even bother programming the address into my cuff.

I wrench open the door and hurry to the lift. If I can escape the ARC and make it here to Hope, I'm fairly certain I can find my way to school. Besides, with Beth already gone, there's nothing I'd like more than to show her I can get to school just fine without her help.

When I get outside I have to ask three different people before I find someone who knows the directions, which are, as luck would have it, fairly straightforward.

After three wrong turns and a near death experience—me *stupidly* forgetting to look before crossing a road, causing a bright red car to screech to a halt centimetres from taking me out—I notice other students heading in the same direction. I must be close, so I follow them the last leg.

The school is a series of dull concrete buildings. A wire fence lines the perimeter and over the entrance gate hangs the slightly askew sign, 'East Hope High'.

After asking a few students, I manage to find my way to the front office, which happens to be nowhere near the front of the school. The office is quite homey, despite the prison like style of building it's in. The walls are covered in notices and a desk stretches across the room, with several wire baskets filled with mounds of paper. Behind the desk sits a small, middle-aged woman. She's wearing a thick sweater in the same grey hue of all my old ARC clothes, which immediately makes me a little homesick.

'Can I help you?' The woman asks, peering up at me over her glasses.

'My name is Elle Winters and I'm meant to be starting here today.'

She looks to her computer screen. 'Yes. I have you registered.'

Her fingers whisk over the keyboard. 'I'll just get your timetable up,' she mutters, more to herself than to me. 'If you could bump your cuff against the CommuSensor please.' She points to the blue glowing sensor on the side of the computer.

I bump my cuff gently against it then hold my arm up to my face to read my timetable, which is now displayed along the clear surface of the cuff.

'Your locker number is 87 and your buddy is Marissa Langley. She should be meeting you just outside the office door to show you around today.' I nod and wait for her to continue.

'You can go now,' she adds.

'Oh, okay. Thanks.' I walk out to the front of the office and look around for Marissa. Most of the students are milling over by one of the other buildings, on a large grass mound. There are no girls even slightly close to the office door.

I walk a little further down the side of the building, lean my back against the wall and look down at my timetable. I have English for the first block of the day. I'm terrible at English, so I'm hoping the school doesn't have high expectations when it comes to the subject.

After that it looks like I have biology, then a session of physical education in the afternoon. I hadn't realised I'd need sports clothes today. Hopefully it won't matter too much.

The bell rings and I look up from my timetable. The 'buddy' still hasn't shown up. I glance around helplessly. I have absolutely no idea where my locker is, let alone where I can find English, in room N4. Whatever that means.

A girl walks around the corner of the building and comes towards me. She's tiny, with a massive mop of brown hair and warm brown eyes, and a complexion that is still very pale. Her skin-tight black jeans, plain white tee, blazer and cute black ankle boots combo makes me wish I'd paid more attention to Quinn's fashion magazines.

'Hi,' she says, as she approaches. 'Are you a newbie?'

'Hey, yeah I'm starting today. You must be Marissa.'

She frowns and slowly shakes her head. 'No. I'm Lara. Is Marissa your buddy? I wouldn't wait around for too long. Marissa isn't the kind of person who'd actually turn up to show around a newbie.'

'Oh.' I feel my heart sink. There aren't *that* many buildings. I'm sure I'll be able to figure it out ... eventually.

'Your name is...' the girl prompts.

'Oh sorry, it's Elle.'

'It looks like I'll be seeing you around Elle.' She begins to walk off.

'Hey, uh, Lara? You wouldn't by chance be able to tell me where English in, um, N4 is?' She stops and turns back to me.

'Nielson building, room four. It's that building over there,' she points to a building in the distance, 'and room four is on the bottom level.'

'Thanks. You're a life saver.'

'It's no hassle. I have English too. I can show you the way if you like?'

'That'd be great.' We walk towards the building in the distance.

'I guess since you ended up here you're an untalent?' she asks.

'I guess,' I say, not feeling all too comfortable delving into my complete lack of talent. 'I don't really see what the big deal is about it all though.'

'Really?' She sounds intrigued. 'Those are big words for a newbie. *Most* people who say stuff like that are just jealous.'

'I guess I'm not *most* people then.'

'Interesting,' she says. I shrug in return. There's nothing wrong with being normal.

'You're pretty you know,' she says, unexpectedly.

'Oh,' I reply, feeling embarrassed. 'Um, thanks?' I continue, unable to come up with an adequate response.

'You must have a boyfriend back in your ARC,' she assumes.

'Not really,' I confess. I'm not certain Sebastian counts as a boyfriend, and he's definitely no longer in the ARC.

'Are you going to ask me if I'm a talent?' she says, rapidly changing the conversation again.

'I thought everyone out here was an untalent?' I venture.

'Most are, but there are different degrees and there are always some that slip through the cracks.'

'Oh.'

'Are you going to ask?' she persists.

'I don't really ' I sigh and scratch my head, 'Does it really matter?' I don't even know this girl.

She laughs in response. 'You're *really* not going to fit in here. Your talent status is everything. Less talent, pretty much equals less friends.'

I guess I will have none then.

'Nnnnn four,' she trumpets, waving her arm at the door. I look up at it, surprised we're here so quickly. Lara pushes through the door before me.

Here goes nothing.

When we enter the room, the class has already begun. My eyes do an automatic sweep of the room for Sebastian, but I already know he's not here. All of the student's eyes are on me, and I look down at my feet as I follow Lara to a couple of empty seats.

As I sit I can still feel people watching me. There's nothing I hate more than too much attention. Especially when it makes me feel more like some strange, freak exhibit than an actual person.

The teacher doesn't register we're late, or if he does he doesn't seem to care. He's an older man who keeps his back to the class, mostly scribbling on the whiteboard.

I pull out my tablet and type the date across the top of the screen. It feels so bizarre to be above ground and sitting in an English class. I almost feel like this couldn't possibly be happening and I've landed in some strange alternate universe.

I sneak a glimpse around the room at the other students, my new classmates I guess I should call them. None of them are particularly interested in the class. Several are whispering to each other, others are giggling at the back of the classroom. At least most of them have lost interest in me.

My eyes fall on one girl who stares intently at her hand, which she holds out in front of her face. I nearly drop my tablet when a spark shoots from her finger like a mini firework and pops in the air, vanishing as quickly as it appeared. She squeals with delight before whispering to the girl next to her, asking if she saw what happened.

I turn to the board at the front of the classroom, trying to stop tears from welling in my eyes. These kids look so carefree and happy and it makes me miss my friends back at the ARC so much. Gemma would always sit through English with me and it's horrible she's not here.

I try to concentrate on the teacher, as he begins to explain the structure of the poem he's written on the board. I look down at my screen to take some notes, but it's no longer blank. Instead it has, in massive scrawl, written across the entirety of the screen, the word 'Hi!'

I instinctively freeze, and then slowly look up and around at the people sitting in class. This is my first direct encounter with any sort of talent and it has me feeling completely uneasy. No one is looking at me so I can't fathom who did it. I look back down at the page and the writing has disappeared.

Great! Now I'm delusional *and* paranoid. I focus back on the teacher. He wants us to write our own poetry this week and tells us we can use the rest of this lesson to begin.

I spend ages trying to think of what I could possibly write about, but I'm at a loss. I prop my head against my hand and stare down at the empty screen in front of me. The only thing worse than having no poetry, is being required to stand up in a class of strangers and tell them anything I do come up with. It's like some form of teenage torture.

From out of nowhere words begin to appear on the screen in front of me. They are scrawled and messy and appear gradually, letter by letter, as if written by an invisible hand.

'Roses are red, violets are blue...' I slam my tablet cover shut over the screen and look around. The words make me nervous and slightly scared. I hadn't expected to see anything even close to the abilities shown in Talented here at school.

The bell chimes outside, and not a minute too soon. I gather my things and quickly head out the door before anything else strange can happen to me. I don't even know where I'm heading as I exit the classroom. I just know I need to get out.

'Hey,' Lara says, catching up with me. 'What's the rush?'

'I just needed to get out of there.'

'Yeah, English with Mr. Morris is the worst. What have you got next?'

I scroll through the timetable on my cuff. 'Biology,' I say, when I find it.

'I can show you where it is if you like?'

'That would be great!' I follow her out from under the building alcove and onto the quadrangle. 'Lara? Do people ever make phantom notes appear on your tablet?'

'Oh, was Hunter doing that to you already?'

'Who?' I ask. She looks around before pointing out a couple of guys, chatting with a group of girls.

'Hunter Blake. He's the tall guy with the dirty blonde hair, kinda turquoise blue eyes, looks like he belongs on Talented...' Looking over, I recognise him. It's the guy who I'd passed the football to last night in the park. He abruptly stops laughing and looks up, catching me watching. I'm lost for a second in the light blue depths of his eyes, but I quickly look away.

'Yeah, I can see the one,' I mutter.

'That's Hunter. He's completely full of himself, which only seems to make the girls like him more.' She rolls her eyes as though she can't for the life of her understand why. 'I mean, what girl can deny a hot jerk?'

I want to say I can, but for a moment I ponder if I would really want to deny someone like Hunter Blake. I quickly shake my head and dismiss the thought. Any girl would be crazy to go for that type of thing.

'He's obviously talented. Why hasn't he been recruited?' I ask.

'I'm not sure,' she says. 'Which is surprising really, as people who show off normally get recruited. The recruiters come through here once a month searching for any talents that may have been missed by the blood analysis, or that have developed more than expected.'

'And you think Hunter should be recruited?' I surmise. I sneak a look back over to where he was standing, but he's no longer there.

'Pretty much.'

'If all this talent stuff is so important. Why are you even talking to me? I'm fairly certain I'm as untalented as they come.' Even that's an understatement.

She considers this for a second. 'I guess because I'm not like most people either. Besides, us untalents have to stick together,' she says, linking her arm through mine.

LARA LEAVES me at the entrance to biology and races off to her history class. I take a second to gather myself before entering the room. Taking deep breaths, I try to relax. Hopefully this class goes better.

As I push the door open my eyes are drawn to the far right corner of the room and I have to stop myself from groaning. I have biology with Beth.

She looks surprised to see me, but is quick to cover her disbelief with a mocking grin. She whispers to the girl sitting at the bench next to her, who lifts her eyes to look at me and starts laughing. I look away to find a seat, hoping she didn't catch the hurt I failed to conceal in my eyes.

I choose one of the tables to the far left of the room, unpack my things and take a seat. I focus down on my tablet, waiting for the class to start.

'You can't sit there,' a deep male voice comes from behind me.

'I'm sorry.' I turn to apologise and find Hunter standing there, looking down at me seriously. Beth laughs and I take a fleeting glance at her. The way she's looking at me, it's clear I'm the butt of her joke. I sigh and turn back to the table.

'I'll just be one second.' I say, gathering my stuff. *Could this day get any worse?*

Hunter bursts into laughter behind me 'I'm kidding,' he says, patting me on the shoulder.

'Right. Funny,' I respond. I feel a bit embarrassed for not realising he was messing around. He laughs again and takes the seat at the table next to me.

'I ... ah.' I really don't want this guy sitting next to me, but what will I say, 'that seat's taken?' I look back at my tablet lying on the table.

'Actually,' he says, getting his own tablet out, 'my mate Trav usually sits where you are, but you're way cuter, so I'm sure he'll understand.'

'Um. Thanks?' I look back at him. 'But your friend is more than welcome to sit here. I can move.' He waves his hand at me as if to say it's no problem.

'I'm Hunter by the way.'

'Elle—'

'Winters,' he interrupts. 'I know.' Lara was right. This guy's totally cocky.

I frown and look away from him. 'So, *Hunter*, are you planning on spending *this* lesson distracting me as well?' I ask.

'I see I'm not the only one who's done their homework,' he says.

I can feel my cheeks become warm with embarrassment. 'I wasn't checking up on *you* specifically. I was just seeing which idiot had been messing around with my tablet.' The corners of his lips pull into a smile. 'So, will you do it again?'

'You'll just have to wait and see...'

Can't wait. I look away from him and bite down on my lip. I have so many responses to what he's said, but I don't want to provoke him into subjecting me to his weird talent all lesson, so I stay silent.

A woman walks in and effectively silences the general hubbub of the classroom. She walks to the front of the room and starts the lesson. Cell structure. Thankfully it's something I know but as the lesson begins and the teacher delves into explanations of tainted cell mutations I feel overwhelmed.

I guess I didn't know that much about cells after all.

I nervously look down at my tablet when I need to begin taking notes. What a surprise, Hunter's composed another message on it.

'You're cute when you're flustered,' is written across the screen. I feel my cheeks flush again. I don't want him to know how bothered I am by his little display. I nudge him really hard with my elbow and the writing disappears. He chuckles beside me.

Luckily he decides to concentrate for the remainder of the lesson and doesn't bother me with anymore of his notes. When the lesson ends I leave the table without saying anything to Hunter.

It's a relief to get back outside. I felt tense all class, not knowing when Hunter would start messing with me again.

'Where you going Winters?' Hunter asks, coming up behind me.

'Ah, lunch?' As soon as I say it though, I realise I don't know where the cafeteria is. He smiles when he sees the confusion on my face, puts his hands on my shoulders and starts steering me.

'If you'd wanted a lunch date with me Winters, all you had to do was ask.'

CHAPTER SIX

The cafeteria is filled with students. It provides a stark contrast to the school dining hall in the ARC, which had a lot fewer students to cater for. For every person there was in the ARC there must be ten people walking around on the surface.

I follow Hunter to queue for food. As I walk across the room to the line I can feel people watching me like there's something wrong with me, like I'm a freak. I try to ignore their stares and keep reminding myself it's only because I'm the new kid. They'll be over it tomorrow—I hope.

As we get closer, and I get a better look at what's being served, I become excited for lunch. The bland food I'm used to in the ARC is nowhere to be seen. Instead, there's an entire buffet of sumptuous smells and enticing looking meals. There's a series of deserts that look mouth watering, not to mention all the fresh fruits and salads. I have no idea what half the stuff is, but I'm more than ready to give it all a try. I find my plate quickly fills and as I look down at it I ponder exactly how I will manage to fit it all in.

'Hungry?' Hunter asks from beside me.

'More intrigued than hungry. I don't know what half the stuff I have is. I mean, look at this,' I point to a yellow blob on my plate, 'No idea!'

'That, Winters, is a lemon tart,' he explains, leaning his mouth in close to my ear.

'Elle!' Lara calls to me from her seat at one of the tables. She waves me over enthusiastically and I go to join her, grateful for the escape. I don't want Hunter to see how much he's managing to get under my skin.

Lara is sitting with another girl and a boy, and as I set my tray down on the table she introduces me.

'Elle, this is Sophie and James. Guys, meet the newbie, Elle.'

'Hey,' they both chime at me in unison. They both have the most unusual eyes, almost a shade of lilac in colour. They would have to be related. Unless their eye colour is a tainted thing?

'They're twins,' Hunter says, pulling out the chair next to me. I whip my head around to look at him and quickly move to sit myself. Was I staring at them *that* obviously?

'You didn't think you were getting away from me that easy did you Winters?' I shrug and give him a look that says, 'I tried.'

'And after asking me here on a lunch date...' He shakes his head and tuts.

'Making friends?' Lara asks me.

'Yeah, unwanted ones,' I say.

Hunter slings his arm over my shoulders. 'Oh don't tell me you don't want me. You'll break my heart.' I try to keep a straight face, but when I look up at him he's giving me the most ridiculous puppy dog eyes and I burst out laughing.

I wiggle my shoulders out from under him.

'Why are you sitting with us?' Sophie asks. 'He never sits with us...' she explains to me, as though he's not even here.

'I was curious as to whether Winters' eyes were bigger than her belly,' Hunter responds with a shrug.

'My eyes and belly are just fine thanks,' I mutter down into my food.

'So, Elle, are you talented?' Sophie asks me.

'No,' I respond, quickly taking a mouthful of food so I don't have to go into any further detail.

Sophie watches me expectantly. Eventually she says, 'Aren't you going to ask us if we're talented?'

'Uh,' I hesitate, looking to Lara who laughs at my response.

'You're supposed to care...' she whispers in my ear, once Sophie and James wipe the astounded looks off their faces and begin chatting with each other.

'Sorry,' I reply. 'I'll keep that in mind.'

'I'm not phased, but others might be...'

I glance over at Hunter as she says this. He's chatting with another guy who's sitting on the other side of him, and for a moment I wonder how phased he is about other people's talents. He doesn't seem to care about anything but himself.

'Which ARC are you from Elle?' James asks.

'I don't know,' I respond, puzzled. I hadn't really thought about the ARC as having an individual identifying name.

'What was the symbol for it?' Sophie asks.

'There was a circle and inside it were two wavy lines, one over the other. Kind of like this.' I trace my fingers along the table to show them.

'That must be Aquarius,' James says, and recognition flares on their faces.

'That's so cool. It's been ages since we've had anyone from there,' Sophie says. 'I hear you guys have a seriously decked out ARC; industry grade hydroponics, libraries, fitness centres...'

'I heard they were even able to modify CommuCuffs for everyone down there,' Lara pipes in. They look at me expectantly.

'I guess we had all that. Don't the other ARCs have similar stuff?'

'Not even close,' Lara says. 'Yours is the biggest.'

'I heard there were a few in Europe that were a similar size,' says Sophie.

'Yeah, but we never hear much about them, it's not like anyone

57

who surfaces over there ends up here. Like Joseph would allow that!' James replies.

I feel Hunter's body go rigid beside me and I glance at him to find he's stopped talking and is staring at James. When he catches me watching, he quickly continues chatting to his friend as though nothing's wrong.

'Does that mean there are other cities on the surface?' I ask, turning back to the others.

'There are only three so far,' Lara explains, gently. She can obviously see I'm feeling overwhelmed. 'They've managed to get one city here, Hope, one in Europe and one in Asia back up and running, well, semi-running. The winters are much longer now, even with the use of The Sphere tech, so there are still a lot of issues with powering everything seeing as so much was reliant on the sun before impact. Winter still dominates most places, so they haven't had much luck elsewhere.'

I nod along as I listen to Lara's explanation, not completely understanding all of what she's said, but enough to get the basic gist of things. It sounds as though they're nowhere close to getting Hope running well enough to allow everyone above ground.

'And who's Joseph?' I ask.

'The guy in charge up here.'

'Right...' I look down into my hands as James begins talking about new technologies they're developing to help reduce the effects of the impact winter in the cities still gripped by it. I can almost feel the weight of the conversation on top of me. It's all too much. I've only just gotten used to the idea of a world going on above the ARC, let alone the fact there's more than one ARC and more than one city up here.

I barely know these people and they all talk about this stuff so easily. It makes me feel so ignorant when I listen to them. Like I've been living under a rock my whole life—which I guess I essentially have been.

'Having fun?' Hunter asks. I turn to him, relieved to have a distraction from the whole ARC conversation.

'Yep.'

He raises his eyebrows at me. Apparently I haven't fooled him 'It's okay to feel overwhelmed by it all. Everyone's in the same boat when they surface. You'll get used to it.'

'I'm fine. Really,' I emphasise. I look away from him though as I say it. I've only just met the guy and yet he seems to know exactly how I feel.

'What have you got after lunch?' he asks.

'PE.'

'I have special studies, so I guess I'll just have to look forward to seeing you tomorrow then.'

'I guess,' I respond. I can feel myself frowning slightly as I look at him. What's his deal?

The bell rings and everyone starts slowly making their way out of the cafeteria.

'What have you guys got now?' I turn to look back to the others as Hunter quickly disappears to class.

'Maths.' James cringes.

'PE.' Sophie grimaces.

'Physical Eeeducation,' Lara sings, causing us all to chuckle.

'I have PE too,' I say.

'Well, we better get a wriggle on.' Lara links her arm through mine and almost drags me out of the room.

'I don't have the right gear. Do you think it'll matter?'

'You'll be fine,' Lara replies. 'They're normally pretty lenient on the newbies, so you'll probably get to sit this one out. Lucky duck. I *wish* I wasn't about to go into a torture session.'

'Torture? How bad is it?' I ask.

'I'm totally exaggerating. It's really not that bad. What are we doing again at the moment?' Lara asks Sophie.

'Netball.'

'I *hate* netball,' Lara groans.

'Yeah, I'm more of a basketball player,' I admit.

'Really?' Lara asks. 'Are you sure?'

'Yes.'

'You just don't seem tall enough,' she responds, sizing me up.

'She doesn't have to be tall to enjoy it,' Sophie says.

'I know. I was just saying,' Lara replies, defensively.

The girls lead me to a set of outdoor courts. There are several students hanging around on them, waiting for the teacher to show up. I'm relieved when I don't find Beth scowling at me from the crowd, eyeing me like I'm the enemy. It's hard enough to deal with her coldness toward me at the Mason's, let alone at school.

When the teacher finally arrives she allows me to keep score for today. Once I'm settled, I find I'm really enjoying the class. It's warm outside and sitting in the sunshine scoring the game is relaxing. A lot of the other girls act reluctant to have to chase the ball around the court, but I'm really quite jealous. I've never been able to play sport outside in the fresh air and under the bright glow of the sun.

Sophie is substituted off and comes to sit next to me.

'Is it true what Lara said? You know, that you're an *untalent*.' She says the word with distaste, and I can't be certain whether she's asked a question or stated fact.

'I'm most definitely not a talent,' I reply. 'And isn't everyone here untalented?'

Her disinterested eyes drift back to watch the game. 'Could be worse,' she says, ignoring my question. 'At least you haven't ended up *talentless* and in the west.'

'Talentless?'

'Yeah, the talentless are the worst, but we try not to think about them. You really shouldn't make a big deal about how untalented you are if you want any friends around here.'

'I don't understand,' I respond. Who are these talentless people? Why haven't I heard of them yet?

'Everyone knows the more talented you are the better your life up here will be. You'll get a good job and will be admired by everyone.

Being talented is pretty much your ticket to a normal life on the surface. Why wouldn't you want to surround yourself with people like that?'

'No, I mean I don't understand about the talentless. Why are they called that?'

'Oh, they're level ones who've been affected by the mutation, but have absolutely no talent. They all live in the West. We don't really talk about them too much. What level are you?'

'I'm not sure...'

'I'm a level four, but my talent's improved so much over the last few months, and with the extra special studies classes I've picked up this term, I might just get recruited one day,' she says, sounding like she'd do anything to be recruited.

She lowers her voice. 'I think if Lara tried harder in special studies she'd have a chance at improving her level and maybe getting recruited, but she doesn't seem to want it.'

'Why not?' I ask.

Sophie goes to respond but the teacher blows her whistle and her time off is over.

Before she heads back on court Sophie pauses, leans in and lightly touches my wrist. 'If I were you I'd be careful around Hunter Blake. He can't be trusted...'

'What?'

The teacher blows her whistle again. 'Chat time is over girls. On court now Sophie!'

I attempt to go back to my quiet enjoyment of the sunshine, but my mind is buzzing after talking to Sophie. If being talented were so important why wouldn't Lara want to be recruited? Why is this the first I've heard of the talentless? And why doesn't she trust Hunter?

When the lesson eventually ends I try to talk to Sophie again, but she rushes off. Lara and I make our way through the school to the entrance I'd come through this morning.

'How was your first day?' Lara asks. I hitch my bag up higher on my shoulder and turn back to look at the dull grey buildings that house the school's classrooms.

'Not as bad as I'd expected,' I say, though I have certainly come out of school with more questions than I went in with.

We walk out the front gate and onto the sidewalk. There are kids everywhere at this hour, streaming steadily onto the street as they rush to escape the confines of school.

'I'm off this way,' Lara says, pointing in one direction.

I hesitate as I attempt to remember the way I'd come from this morning. The buildings by the school all look so similar and I'd been in such a rush on my way here I barely remember any of the walk. I look around hoping maybe Beth would've waited, but she's nowhere to be seen.

I sigh and bring up the Mason's address on my cuff. I'm still not the best at using the tracking function, but I should be able to find my way eventually.

'Oh, you're in apartment block E54, that's right by my place,' Lara says, peering at my cuff from over my shoulder. 'You're staying barely even two blocks from me. C'mon, we can walk together.'

'Thanks,' I say. This girl has saved me so many times today, I feel like I could hug her. 'Sorry to put you out. This wouldn't be a problem if Beth had just waited for me!'

'Don't be silly. It's no problem... Hang on. You live with Beth Mason?' she asks.

'Yeah. She's in the family I was fostered to.'

'You were fostered out? That sucks. You must miss your family.'

'I never really had a family,' I mumble. 'But I do miss my friends. My best friend Quinn and I are practically sisters. Her not being here; it kind of feels like a piece of me is missing.'

'I know exactly what you mean,' she says. 'I'm like that about my dad. Things haven't been the same without him.'

We walk in silence, both contemplating those we left behind. I try to imagine what Quinn would be like if she was here and it makes me want to smile. She would've found out half of the student's talents by the end of first period, have five dates lined up by lunch and she'd probably have hatched a plan to find Sebastian by dinner. I miss her cool confidence. I could really use a dose of it up here.

'I'm surprised you live with Beth,' Lara eventually says. 'She's one angry individual.'

'What do you mean?' I ask

Lara thinks for a moment before responding. 'Well look at her... You don't dress like that unless you're seriously pissed off with the world.'

'I'm sure she doesn't hate the world,' I say, coming to her defence. Even after the way she's been treating me, I still find I want to protect her. We'd once been so close and I have to believe the girl I grew up with is still there somewhere.

Lara simply shrugs in response. 'It's just the impression I get.'

We walk for a block in silence before she talks again. 'It looks like Hunter has you in his sights. Do you like him?'

'No,' I reply, a bit too quickly. 'He just sat next to me in biology.'

'He's obviously into you,' she says.

'I have no idea why. I just met the guy and he's really not my type. Besides, there's this guy...' She grabs my arm and stops me still in my tracks.

'There's a guy?' she asks.

'He's more of a friend... I think. He came here just a couple of weeks before me and I've been trying to find him, but I haven't had any luck. I was thinking of going back and asking at the reintegration centre.'

Lara shakes her head. 'Asking them would be about as helpful as asking mud. You won't have any luck with the authorities. They're all too busy with more important tasks and don't particularly care about missing friends.'

'I was worried about that being the case,' I respond, trying not to feel too despondent. I will just have to find another way to get to him.

'What's his name?' she asks.

'Sebastian Scott.'

'Sebastian Scott.' She pauses as she considers the name. 'He's definitely not at East Hope High. I know everyone at East. It's most likely he's in the West Hope sector if he's only been here a few weeks.' Her face darkens as she says this and she hurries to continue walking.

'With the talentless?' I ask, catching up with her.

She hesitates before responding, 'Most likely, I mean, there is the possibility he could be in North Hope. If a kid has a high enough reading in their test they can go straight there. It doesn't happen often, but it does happen.'

'How can I find out for sure?'

'I have a friend who comes over from the west once every so often. I could maybe ask him if he's seen Sebastian.'

'That would be amazing. Would it be easier if I went to West Hope and met him?'

'No, it's best if we wait for him,' she responds.

'How about from North Hope? Do you know anyone we could ask there?'

'No,' she replies. She looks genuinely disappointed she can't help me more.

'Don't worry about it,' I say. 'Hopefully he's in West Hope.' *Please Sebastian be there!* 'When will you talk to your friend?'

'He's supposed to be coming here tomorrow night, hopefully I can ask him then.' We reach the next intersection and Lara stops.

'I'm down this way,' she indicates around the corner, 'you're straight ahead a few blocks.'

'Great. I'll see you at school tomorrow?'

'Yep. Meet me here at about ten past eight if you like and we can walk together again.'

'Sounds good.' I continue walking.

'Oh, here,' she says, stopping me. 'We should bump cuffs just in case one of us is running late.'

'Sure,' I respond.

We nudge our CommuCuffs against each other and I look down at it to check it registered. @LaraTTaylor flashes across the screen.

'Okay, all good,' she says, looking up from hers. 'See you tomorrow.'

Once she's around the corner and out of eyesight I almost jump with excitement. I finally have *something* to go on to find Sebastian.

As I continue on towards the apartment, I begin to feel a sense of optimism stirring inside of me. For the first time since I left the ARC I have a lead. Lara's help isn't a lot to go on, but it's a start.

CHAPTER SEVEN

'Have you heard from your friend?' I ask Lara, in a hushed voice. She looks over at the twins, who are deep in conversation, and then down at her plate again.

'No, he didn't come by last night,' she replies.

My shoulders slouch in response. This is all I've been able to think about since she mentioned it to me, so it's hard to hide my disappointment.

I take a bite of my sandwich. The bread feels dry and tasteless in my mouth, not appealing at all. I place the rest of it back down on my plate.

'Why do you think he didn't come?'

'I'm not sure.' She taps her fingers across her mouth as she thinks. 'Maybe he's struggling to get a pass into East Hope?'

'What do you mean?'

'Anyone travelling between East and West Hope needs to be approved for a day pass. It wouldn't be the first time he's been denied entry.'

I frown in return. 'Are they strict about that?'

'Oh yeah, there's major restrictions. Haven't you seen the wall between East and West?'

I shake my head.

'It's massive.'

'Can't you comm him?' I ask.

'Nope. Doesn't work. Your cuff only registers users in your sector. Convenient, huh?'

'Very,' I respond. I look down at my fingers, which pick aimlessly at the uneaten remains of my sandwich. It's strange they would split the city up in such a way and prohibit movement between the sectors. It gives me a bad feeling.

'How about if we went to see him?' I ask.

She chews down on her lower lip as she considers this. It doesn't look like she finds the option appealing. 'We could...' she wagers.

'I haven't got anything planned this weekend. If you're free, we could go over there tomorrow?'

'Sure,' she says, with a strained smile. Her tightly pulled lips make it clear she isn't happy about my idea at all. Why is she so against the idea of going into the western part of the city?

'Are you excited for your first special studies session?' James asks me.

'Yeah, can't wait,' I say, with half-hearted enthusiasm.

'You shouldn't stress. The lesson is really easy.'

'Okay.' I attempt to inject more excitement into my voice, but I'm not very convincing. I've been worrying about the lesson all week and I'm not doing a very good job at hiding it. From what I've been told, the teacher can sense other people's talents, so I have every reason to worry. I can't let them know the truth about me.

The bell rings and the knots tied in my stomach tighten. I battle with my internal desire to ditch school for the rest of the day. It wouldn't be the first time I've missed a class, but it would be a first on the surface, and I still need to be careful about drawing attention to myself.

Lara stands up and gathers her stuff.

'You coming?' she asks.

'Yeah.' I pick my bag up off the back of my seat and sling it over my shoulder. We shuffle out of the cafeteria behind the twins.

'The lesson will be fine,' Lara reassures me, when we reach the door. 'You can tell me all about it after school.'

'Okay,' I agree, hoping I'm still around to tell her about it once the school day ends.

Lara turns off towards the science labs and I start slowly trudging towards the special studies classroom. I know I'll have to face this lesson at some stage, but it sure would be nice to avoid confronting my potential doom right at this very second. I've barely had a chance to look for Sebastian, and I don't know what I'd do if I was sent back to the ARC so soon. My only hope is the teacher isn't able to tell I have no talent.

When I enter the classroom I don't recognise any of the students from my other classes. I quietly move past them and find a seat in an empty row at the back of the room.

As I take my tablet out I look around at the others in the room. Not one of them has their tablet out and half of them aren't even seated in chairs. Most are sitting or lying on the floor silently with their eyes closed. I get the feeling this class won't be anything like my usual ones.

When the teacher walks in none of the students notice. He's young, maybe in his early twenties? He has long shaggy hair and wears large glasses that magnify his eyes. His clothes are crinkled and baggy, and he's completely different to the other teachers I've met so far—definitely not what I expected. He spots me at the back of the room and walks straight towards me.

'You must be Elle. Could I get you to come with me?' he asks. I look around at the other students nervously. Have I done something wrong?

'Uh, yeah?' I respond. *Like I have a choice.* I jam my tablet into my bag and rush to follow him outside. He takes me over to sit at one of the benches that are perched on the grassy quad, bathed in sunshine.

'I thought we should have a bit of a chat,' he says. 'My name's Mr. Kale and I'm relieving Mr. Finch, who would regularly take this class, for the next couple of months. Before we get you diving right in, I wanted to explain a little of what we do in this lesson.

'You've probably already heard special studies is about learning to access and control your individual talent. For some people their talent comes quite naturally, but for others it can be more difficult to tap into.'

Or impossible, if you're me.

'Essentially, your talent is linked with your ability to focus and internally visualise what it is you want to do. It is different in each and every one of us. Some people are limited by their ability to focus and visualise. Others are limited by the way their genes have mutated. Either way, this class should help make the most of what you can do.'

'I don't know what my talent is,' I say.

'That's okay. Lots of people are still finding their way, and you've been placed in a beginners' stream, so there is no rush at all for now. Today the class is using this time for meditation.'

My eyebrows crease as I strain to comprehend exactly how this works. 'We spend class meditating?' I conclude.

'And visualising,' he adds.

'Okay.' I nod. I have no idea how to do this, but the class sounds like a breeze. I shouldn't find it too difficult to sit around daydreaming every Friday afternoon. I'm almost lucky Gemma isn't here though; we pretty much got detention every Friday for the entire month our class did yoga in PE last year. We'd spent every lesson laughing as we attempted the crazy yoga poses, and it only got worse when we were expected to sit and meditate. I can't imagine Mr. Kale would take to that too kindly.

'Take my hands,' he says.

'What?' I respond, drawing my hands closer.

'Take my hands,' he repeats. I cautiously put my hands in his, not certain I feel comfortable with it.

'I'm going to try and do a reading on you. Find out where your aptitude lies, so we can attempt to mould you appropriately.'

'You want to do what to me?'

He ignores my question, closes his eyes and takes in several deep breaths. This is a bad idea. I should've skipped. What was I thinking?

'I can see you've had a lot of turmoil in your life,' he mumbles, like a bad fortune-teller. Normally I would've found it hard not to snigger, but I'm starting to get worried. What if he can tell I'm not like everyone else here?

'Yes,' he continues. 'You've spent a long time alone, you were abandoned when you were very young.'

My blood turns cold. 'How... How do you know that?'

'You lost someone close to you recently and I can see how much you're struggling with it.'

I hold my breath, waiting for his next sentence. Is he talking about Sebastian?

'But you don't have to worry. He's close.' I grip his hands tighter and move forward to the edge of my seat. If he knows where Sebastian is I have to get it out of him. I wait for him to continue, but he's silent for several minutes.

'Where is he?' I barely whisper.

He opens his eyes and looks at me, confused. 'I can't see ... usually I'd be able to see...'

'What's wrong?' I ask. My concern grows as his brow furrows further. I'm pretty certain I already know what he will say.

'I can't see anything to do with any talent. It's almost like you haven't even got one.' My heart falters in its beating.

He knows.

'Could it be it's just very, very weak?' I ask.

He slowly shakes his head as he considers this option. 'No, I don't think...'

I clutch my hand to my chest. I can barely breathe. Everything

I've gone through has been for nothing. What am I going to do?

'I mean, I guess it's a possibility,' he eventually says. But when I look at him closely it's obvious he's doubtful that's the answer. Then his eyes clear up.

'No, you're right. I guess there are some people even I can't read. I am very sorry for you though, with you having *such* a lack of talent. You will find it very hard adjusting to life here and will have to work extraordinarily hard in special studies to improve.'

'It's okay,' I say, my body sagging with relief. 'Can I go back to class now?'

He nods in response. 'Just please see that you do work hard on your special studies. It's very important.'

'I'll try my best,' I assure him, before escaping back to class.

Once I'm back at my desk, I close my eyes and pretend to meditate, or whatever it is we're supposed to be doing. My hands are shaking, so I take deep steady breaths. That had been incredibly close.

I wish I'd realised there were people who could read me in such a way. How had he known I was an orphan? What had he seen about Sebastian? I open my eyes and look at him sitting at his desk.

Could he help me find Sebastian? He'd been suspicious about my lack of talent though, so I want as little contact with this man as possible. Even if he found out about me, what could they do? They can't exactly put me back in the ARC now I know about all of this.

I put my head down in my hands. If they can't put me back in the ARC, it means I can't bring Sebastian home with me.

We can't go back.

The words repeat in my mind over and over and tears form in the corners of my eyes. There had always been the possibility I wouldn't return to the ARC. No one else has ever gone back, why would I? But, it's so clear now the reason behind the one-way trip.

I subtly wipe under my eyes with my fingers and check to make sure no one's seen. The other students are thoroughly immersed in meditation, but I catch Mr. Kale watching me, clearly concerned. I shut my eyes again trying to block him out.

No matter which way I look at it, I can't accept this is okay. If we can't go back, it means I'll never see Quinn again, or any of the others; and they'll never know about the surface.

When the bell rings for the end of the day I don't wait for Lara. I slip a note in her locker telling her I'll see her tomorrow morning. I can't handle walking home with her now, trying to pretend every thing's okay when it's not. Not today.

When I arrive out front of the apartment building I look up at it and then quickly look away. Cathy would be home and she'd be her usual perky self. I know she's just trying to make my adjustment as easy as possible, but I can't handle her enthusiasm today.

A leaf blows down onto the ground in front of me and I think of the park I'd walked to the other day. Yes, that's the perfect place to go.

ONCE I ARRIVE, I decide not to go too far off course in my wandering. Instead I head to the open grass area I'd seen people relaxing on the other day. It's quite light outside, so when I get there I'm not surprised people are lazing around on the grass, enjoying the last hours of sunshine for the day.

In the middle of the field is a lone tree that offers some inviting shade. I walk towards it and sit in the cool cover of its canopy.

It's relaxing here and I lie back on the grass. I stare up at the way the sun dances through the leaves in the branches above. It's beautiful—almost hypnotic.

If I have lost my friends forever, and have no choice but to start over, maybe somewhere like here wouldn't be so bad? I exhale and close my eyes, allowing myself to appreciate the breeze playing softly across my skin, the smell of grass tingling in my nose. For a moment I'm able to forget about the life I've left behind in the ARC and just live and breathe for this very instant.

My eyes feel heavy and despite my worry I gently fall asleep.

I AWAKE to the sound of strangled moans whimpering from my throat. My entire body is frozen with terror, as though it is still within the icy grasp of my nightmare.

I attempt to jerk my body upwards, to sit up. But the reaction is more sluggish than expected. My head spins as I sit fully upright. I can still sense the presence of the dream. It's eerie and foreboding. The feeling gathers around me like a thick coat of frost, chilling me to the core.

I shudder and swiftly wipe away the moisture I can feel under my eyes.

The nightmare had been so real.

I struggle as I try to remember the details that moments ago had been so clear. It had felt so important.

I shake my head, frustrated. I can't remember...

A fragment cuts through the fog and into my memory. Quinn... Quinn had been in it. She'd been in danger.

I try to remember why she was in danger, but the details slip further from my grasp. I rub my face, sleepily. It's not like the dream matters. If anything it probably means I'm in desperate need of a good night's sleep.

I wrap my arms around my knees and pull them to my chest. I feel cold and slightly nauseas. My head is pounding. It's as though several death metal bands have taken up residence inside it and are jumping around as they play their loudest set.

I stand and pat the grass off my pants as I walk away from the tree. I move quickly, wanting to distract myself from the raucous concert in my head. I'm walking so determinedly, so desperately trying to get as far away from my nightmare as possible, that I slam straight into someone.

'Sorry,' I mutter.

'Elle?'

I look up and Hunter is frowning down at me.

He takes a hold of both my arms. 'Elle, you're as white as a ghost. Are you alright?'

'I'm fine.' I push out of his grasp to walk on.

'You don't look fine...' he says, following me.

'I said I'm fine Hunter.'

He looks shocked at my irritation, but quickly gets over it. 'Are you sick?' he asks. I shake my head. 'Wait no, don't tell me ... you're lovesick. You missed me so much at lunch today you're physically ill.'

'You know you're impossible,' I groan.

'Don't pretend you don't love it.'

I want to roll my eyes at him, but can't stand the idea of giving him any more attention—like his massive ego needs it.

'Don't you have other girls you could be busy irritating? From what I've seen you're very popular with the girls at school.'

'Are you jealous?' he asks.

I raise my eyebrows at him in response. 'Yeah, you got me, totally jealous.'

'No need to be quite so sarcastic...' He acts like he's offended, but then laughs. 'And just so you know, I'd much rather be irritating you than some other girls.'

'Great,' I mutter.

'Seriously though, are you okay? You really didn't look okay before.'

'It was just a headache. I'm fine,' I insist. 'Do you come to the park often?' I ask, before he can probe me any further.

'Pretty much every day. It's a nice place to escape it all.'

'Definitely,' I agree. It's the nicest place I've ever been, but I'm too embarrassed to tell him that.

My cuff starts vibrating. I look down at it and see an incoming comm from Lara.

'You going to get that?' Hunter asks, as I stare at it.

I shake my head. 'Nah, I'll comm her back later.' The last thing I want to do is have a conversation with Lara about our trip to West Hope in front of Hunter.

We walk in silence for a while, just taking in the scenery. It's kind of pleasant.

'What's it like?' I ask. 'You know ... being special?'

'Being talented? I dunno. I guess it's cool being able to do things others can't. But it just feels natural. Like talking or walking. Just a part of who you are, if that makes sense.'

'How long have you been talented?'

'When I first came up here, four years ago, I was pretty untalented. It just developed as I grew older.'

'I've heard you're going to be recruited.'

'I hope not,' he scoffs.

'That's not what you're aiming for?'

'That's the last thing I want,' he says. 'I'm not getting recruited, and I'm not going to the other side of the river. But, at the same time, I won't deny who I am and I want to be the best I can be. Part of that is developing my talent. So, I find ways to avoid recruitment.'

'Ways?'

'*Ways*,' he says, winking at me.

I shake my head. Who would've thought he'd considered this stuff. 'You were almost coming off as thoughtful there for a moment.'

'It has been known to happen.' He laughs quietly at himself.

When the river appears up ahead I stop. I hadn't realised how far we'd walked. 'I should probably head back,' I say. 'It seems to get dark so quickly up here.'

'I'll walk you home.'

I stare at him, slightly too stunned by his statement to respond. This guy is renowned at school for being a cocky ass and we've just had a long, somewhat pleasant, conversation. Now he wants to walk me home? Why's he being so nice?

He starts to walk back the way we came. 'You coming?' he yells, tossing the words over his shoulder.

'Yeah, sorry.' I shake off the daze. As I jog to catch up with him I get an uneasy feeling and Sophie's warning about him comes to mind. He's being *too* nice. What could he possibly want with me?

CHAPTER EIGHT

'Sorry I'm late,' Lara says, rushing towards me.

'I almost thought you weren't going to come,' I reply. It has, after all, been twenty minutes since we were supposed to meet at the small, dingy cafe I've been sitting at.

'Sorry, I got held up at home, should we get going?'

'Definitely.' I don't want to waste another second, not when today could be the day I find Sebastian. Plus, this place gives me the creeps.

I stand up, but sway unsteadily on my feet as I take a step towards Lara.

'Are you alright?' she asks, rushing over.

I stand still for a moment, before I respond. 'Sorry, head rush,' I laugh. 'I'm fine.'

'Are you sure?'

'Will you stop worrying? I'm fine. I swear.'

She holds her hands up. 'Okay, okay.'

Lara catches my expression, as I eye the place up as we leave, and laughs. 'I could probably have picked a better meeting place, but this was the first spot that came to mind. Mostly because it always creeps me out, which is another good reason we should've met somewhere else.' She laughs again. 'Sorry about that. At least we're only a few blocks from the wall. It shouldn't take us long to get there from here.'

When the towering concrete slab comes into view, I shiver involuntarily at the sight. The wall is huge with thick rings of barbed wire running across the top of it. Even under the bright sun, that shines high overhead, the wall looks foreboding.

'Why would they put this up?' I ask Lara, lowering my voice as we pass two older ladies.

'Everyone in the West, East and North of Hope have slightly different mutations, which is the supposed reason they separate us all. Because the mutation is something so new, they want to be able to monitor what is happening and to do so they've divided the city.'

'And they built a wall this large to do that?'

'Apparently.'

As we move closer to the wall, we fall in line behind several people queuing to visit the other side. The line isn't too long and it moves relatively quickly. Lara continuously twists the bracelet she's wearing around her wrist. The closer we get to the gate, the more agitated her movement becomes.

'Are you okay?' I ask her, when we're a few people away from the front of the line.

She peers over her shoulder to the others who wait behind us. 'Can't you see how tense everyone is?'

I follow her line of sight. The faces around us are serious, yes, but they don't appear nearly as tense as Lara is. I can't bring myself to tell her she's overreacting though.

'Next.' A guard at the gate beckons us forward. He quickly passes a scanner over our cuffs.

'Remember to abide by the curfew in West Hope,' the man warns. 'You have 24 hours here before you'll need to report back to the gate and leave or extend your pass.'

I glance at Lara to gauge her reaction to what the man's said, but she's staring straight ahead, refusing to make eye contact.

Once we've been ushered through the gate and are out of earshot

I ask her about the curfew. Her answer is lost on me though, as I catch a look at the long line of people queuing to visit East Hope.

Most people wear clothes that hang loosely off their bodies and everyone's skin is so pale, you'd swear they only just left the ARC. Too many of the faces that stare bleakly towards the front of the line are gaunt and there's a sombre atmosphere that hangs like a Lycortium tainted cloud over the crowd.

'Why are there so many people?' I ask.

'It's not as simple as getting a scan if you're from West Hope. You have to answer all these questions and fulfil all these medical requirements. It takes a while, hence the line.'

'Why all the questions? What's wrong with them?'

Lara lowers her voice. 'They look that way because of the mutation, because they're talentless. Come on, we should get a move on if we want to find Josh.'

West Hope appears to be very different from the east side of the city. I'm immediately struck by how there are a lot fewer people on this side of the wall, and the whole place is strangely quiet.

The tall, shiny skyscrapers are quick to disappear from view, and are replaced by short, stone buildings that are crumbling and covered with graffiti. Bits of rubbish become more frequent in the streets, and I can't escape the bad smells rising from the potholes on the road.

It becomes increasingly dilapidated until we reach a huge open square that looks onto a pristine, white building. The place is a monstrosity, spanning the distance of several blocks. There are only a few windows visible on the face of it making it appear severe and uninviting.

The garden surrounding it couldn't be more different, with open areas of grass and hedges that have been manicured within an inch of their life. It's a beautiful sight but also incredibly eerie. It is deadly quiet here, sending shivers down my spine.

Lara's eyes briefly flicker towards the large white building before she pulls me in another direction, leading us away. She doesn't say a word and her pace quickens as we head towards a series of small shops.

'What was that place?'

'The hospital.'

'The way you reacted I could've sworn we were walking away from a prison.' To be honest, I don't blame her for her reaction. I got a bad feeling from the place too.

She raises her eyebrows as if to say, 'who says we weren't?' and turns back to focus on the shops ahead. Specifically, she heads towards one of the small restaurants, which has tables out the front with large umbrellas made of faded red material covering them in shade.

'Just try to avoid ever being sick. That isn't a very nice place,' she tells me, before pushing through the door to the restaurant.

There are no customers inside except for a small girl who is sitting up at the bar, at the back of the room. Her face lights up when she turns and sees Lara walking in.

'Lara!' she squeals. She jumps down from her chair and runs towards us with such speed she nearly falls over as she throws her arms around Lara's legs.

'Hey Mia,' Lara responds, smiling and patting her on the head. 'Are you in charge of the place today?'

'Uh huh,' the girl replies. She stands back and looks at us seriously. 'Can I take your order?'

Lara laughs. 'Is your brother around?'

'Josh!' Mia yells, running towards the back of the restaurant. 'Your *girlfriend* is here!' Lara immediately begins to blush when she hears this.

'Which one?' a guy yells back.

'The one you're in *love* with,' Mia says, covering her mouth in an attempt to hide her giggles.

The guy, Josh, emerges from the kitchen. He's wearing an apron that's covered in flour and has a huge smile plastered across his face. 'Hey Lara,' he says.

He opens his arms, as though to give Lara a hug, but then stops dead in his tracks and looks down at the flour on his apron. His smile quickly turns slightly devious and he rushes her, pulling her in for a massive hug.

'Josh!' she yells, squirming to get away from him and the flour that coats her outfit. Her struggles only make him hug her harder and neither of them can stop laughing.

When Lara finally pulls away she thumps his arm hard. 'You're such a dick.'

This only makes his smile broader.

'Elle, this is Josh.'

'Hi,' he says, turning and offering out his hand to me. 'What brings you guys over here?'

I look to Lara for guidance on what to say. She's quick to jump in with a response. 'We're looking for Elle's boyfriend and we were hoping you could tell us if he's here in West Hope? His name is Sebastian Scott.'

I leave the quip about him being my boyfriend alone. I don't know what we are—or were. I should be feeling excited to hear Josh's response but, since arriving in West Hope, I've been praying I won't find Sebastian here after all.

Looking at Josh, he obviously once had an extremely athletic build that is now diminishing. Mia looks like she's never had the chance to grow big and strong. She's so tiny I worry how easily she could get hurt or sick. I wouldn't want that for anyone, let alone Sebastian. I'd rather not find him at all if it meant he could stay healthy.

'I haven't heard the name.' Josh replies. 'He's not at school but that doesn't completely rule out him being in West Hope. Have you thought about contacting M?'

'Who's M?' I ask.

Josh glances at Lara and she gives the tiniest shake of her head. 'Someone who could help,' is all he will say.

I study Lara's face, which is void of any expression. She's holding something back from me, but I have no idea what it could be.

'If he can help, can I meet him?'

'It's not that simple,' Lara explains. 'M isn't someone you just meet up with. We'll have to send a message through to him and hope he'll get back to us. Josh can you do that?'

'I can go now if you like?'

'Would you mind?' Lara asks him.

'What do you think Mia? Would I mind?' he turns and asks the young girl.

Mia enthusiastically shakes her head.

'I guess I don't mind then. Mia you're in charge. Girls, feel free to help yourself to something to drink. I'll be back in a few.' He peels off his apron and tosses it across the back of one of the bar stools before heading out the front door.

I follow Lara to sit at one of the booths by the window while we wait. Lara begins to play with her bracelet again and her attention is focused on the world outside the window—not that there's all that much going on out there.

'How do you know Josh?' I ask her.

'I knew Josh and his sister when we lived in the ARC,' she says, continuing to stare out the window. 'They both came to Hope before me. Mia first, then Josh.'

'How did you find them when you got here?'

'Purely by accident. I came to the west to arrange a meeting with M, to try and contact my dad in the ARC, and bumped into Josh.'

'Were you able to talk to your dad?'

'No,' she says. 'Even M has his limits.'

'Which are?'

She smiles. 'I'm sure he'll be able to help you find Sebastian.'

I try to get her to open up more about what she means, but she completely shuts down. Her answers leave no room for conversation, so I slouch back in the chair and wait for Josh in silence.

He returns almost an hour later and Lara's attention returns with him.

'How did it go?' she asks, as soon as he enters the restaurant.

He shakes his head sadly. 'All I could do was send a message through to him. I'll let Lara know what he says when I hear. Sorry I can't be more help.'

'No, it's okay. Thank you for trying,' I say.

'Anytime. Do you girls want to stay for some food? I was thinking of whipping up my mean vegie pasta for the restaurant tonight.'

'Thanks Josh, but we should probably head back now,' Lara says.

Josh's face falls. I'm surprised Lara isn't more keen to stay. It certainly looks like Josh was hoping she would. Instead, we both begin to move towards the front door.

Josh grabs Lara's arm, stopping her. 'Can I have a quick word with you before you go?' he asks, the playfulness gone from his voice now.

She slowly nods her head and follows him out back. They're only gone for a little while, but when Lara comes back she is even more distracted and quieter than before.

'What did he want?' I ask her, once we've left the restaurant.

'Just to see how I'm going. He worries about me.' Given Josh's condition, he appears to need more worrying about than Lara, but I get the feeling there's a lot more than I'm aware of going on beneath her cool exterior.

'I'm sorry we couldn't find out more about Sebastian,' she says.

'It's okay. I just hope he's not over here. I hate to think of him becoming sick like everyone else.'

Lara watches me uneasily. 'Elle, if he's not here then it's likely he's in the one place you can't go.'

'North Hope. Why won't they let us go there?'

'Because it's against the rules.'

'But why?'

'Because it's dangerous. Look, Josh wasn't certain he's not in the west. Sebastian could still be here. Let's just exhaust all our options before we worry about the north, okay?'

'Like the south side of the city? Could he be there?' I ask.

'Nobody lives there. It's just a bunch of ruins from before...' Lara's voice trails off and she falls silent as the hospital comes into view again. The place isn't quite as deserted as before, but is still shrouded in the kind of silence that leaves you feeling cold.

There's a line of people leading out from one of the side entrances. They're too far away to see their faces clearly, or to over-hear any of their conversations, so I have no idea why they're there. Lara's gone so quiet I doubt I'll be able to get a word out of her until we're on the other side of the wall, let alone answers about why so many people are lining up outside the hospital.

As we move further away from the hospital, I glance back over my shoulder at it and shudder. Sebastian may be in a more dangerous part of the city, but can it really be worse than here?

CHAPTER NINE

'Hi Elle,' Cathy calls out when I enter through the front door.

'Hi Cathy,' I reply, following her voice into the kitchen. She's busy, bent over the stove cooking. I'm hardly surprised. Cathy probably loves cooking as much as she cares about her children. I've barely seen her out of the kitchen since I arrived.

'Did you have fun with your friend?' she asks, looking at me over her shoulder.

'Yes.'

'What did you girls get up to?'

'The usual girl stuff.' I grab an apple from the fruit bowl and head towards the living room. I hate lying to Cathy, and I'm too distracted to be even slightly convincing about it right now. I haven't been able to get the idea of going to the north side of the river out of my head. It has kept me preoccupied all afternoon.

I know Lara said it was dangerous, and maybe she's right, but I can't fathom where else Sebastian could be. It's the only option I haven't explored and I'm just wasting time if I sit here and do nothing.

Anything could be happening to him over there and the longer I put if off the more likely it is I'll be found out. I'm almost certain Mr. Kale is already suspicious I'm completely normal. I need to do something while I still can. Who knows what they'll do to me if I'm found up here without any mutation?

I enter the living room and Beth is sitting on the couch staring out the window. The TV is on, but her mind looks as though it's miles away.

I almost turn and walk straight back out. I hate being caught alone with her. It's always so awkward. I want her to be the friend I once had and I get so disappointed every time she brushes me off.

I sit on one of the other couches and focus on the television. A news reporter is interviewing an expert about another city recently discovered in Australia, that has begun to naturally thaw out. He predicts that with Sphere technology they'll be able to make it liveable within two years.

A squeal comes from Jackson in the kitchen, as Cathy catches him trying to sneak a cookie before dinner. Beth sighs from her spot on the couch. She's not watching the television; instead she's playing with something on her lap.

'Are you ever going to tell me what happened?' I ask.

Her back goes rigid and her face turns hard. 'I don't know what you're talking about.'

She continues to look at whatever it is she's playing with in her lap. She tucks it away in her pocket but, as she does, I catch a glint of light along the metal circumference of a locket. *Her* locket. I can't believe she still has it after all these years. Her mum gave it to her when we were kids and if she still has that, it means she still cares about her family.

'You still have your locket...'

'I don't have anything.'

'Yes you do. I saw it,' I say.

'I don't know what you're talking about,' she says again.

I look back towards the kitchen and nervously grasp the pendant that always hangs around my neck. 'You still care. You're still the girl who was once my best friend.'

'That person is long gone,' she replies. 'You'd better stop looking for her in me. It's a waste of your time and you'll be sadly disappointed.' She looks up at me, no emotion showing on her face. April no longer shines out of her hollow eyes, but I know she's in there somewhere.

'Please won't you reconsider helping me find Sebastian?'

'No,' she says.

'Don't you want to find him?' I ask. Her eyes betray an emotion, but I can't tell whether it's anger, hope, love... I have as much insight into her as a stranger would.

'Who's Sebastian?' Jackson asks, from behind me. Beth stands and glares down at me before walking over and guiding him back to the kitchen.

'He's no one,' she says. 'Just some guy Elle likes to think I'd want to meet. But she's wrong.' She directs her words at me, and I try not to take it to heart. How can she not want to find him?

I turn myself back around on the sofa to look at the television. I hate feeling so helpless when it comes to her. I keep trying to reach out to her, but all she does is push me away.

There's a fit of laughter in the kitchen and I turn to see Beth lift Jackson onto her back and gallop around the room with him. She almost appears happy until she sees me watching. The light slips from her eyes, leaving them empty. I quickly snap my head back around.

LATER THAT NIGHT I lie in bed looking up to the ceiling. My body feels tired, but my mind and heart are racing. I keep thinking about the bridge that leads to the other side of the river. It's almost calling to me.

I groan, thump my pillow and roll onto my side. When I close my eyes I see it clearer than before. It's night and it's lit up in an orange, yellow glow. The lamps that line it reflect down into the calm water, the slightest of ripples gently denting the reflection.

I punch my pillow down again. It's the middle of the night. I can't exactly go across the bridge now in search of Sebastian It'd be completely stupid. I huff out an irritated breath and roll onto my other side.

If only sleep would come to me. I wouldn't keep seeing this damn bridge. I open my eyes and stare out the window. The city lights twinkle in the night sky. The way they're lit up, you'd think the whole place was wide-awake.

I rub my eyes, which feel beyond tired, yet determined to stay awake. Throwing my legs over the side of the bed, I get up and go to the kitchen for some water.

As I stand by the kitchen window, clutching the cold glass to my chest, I feel dwarfed by the sheer size of the city that lies below. There are so many people, how are you supposed to find just one?

I worry the answer is you can't, but quickly push that disturbing thought aside. I will find him. I know it.

I tiptoe back to my room, keeping especially quiet as I move down the hallway past the other bedrooms. The door to Beth's room is slightly ajar. I'm tempted to take a quick peek through the crack to see if she appears so hostile when she sleeps, but can't bring myself to do it. Instead, I take extra care not to make any noise. Waking her up would so not be worth it.

A thud comes from the living room and I stop dead in my tracks, my heart in my mouth. Silence echoes throughout the house. I begin to relax slightly as the seconds tick past and I don't hear another noise. Maybe something fell over out there?

There's a soft creaking of the floorboards nearby and my body seizes up, taught with tension again. I listen carefully, and can just make out the sound of soft and careful footsteps, slowly making their way across the living room.

My mind flutters, trying to figure out how someone has broken into the house. It was deadly quiet when I'd first got up, and the living room had been empty when I'd walked through it a minute ago. Surely I would've seen or heard someone?

The footsteps creep closer. They're almost at the entrance to the hallway now.

Holding my breath, I edge my way towards my bedroom door, terrified to make a noise.

A footstep creaks in the hallway behind me. I freeze again. I'm too scared to look behind me and too scared to move forward. The footsteps stop and are replaced by the slow and steady breaths of the intruder, which are loud in the silent house. They're so close that even in the darkness of the hallway they must be able to see me.

'What are you doing?' Beth's hushed voice spits at me from behind. I jump in reaction and turn as she skulks towards me.

'Me? What are you doing?' I respond, trying to calm my erratically beating heart. Is she trying to scare me to death? 'I was just out in the living room, how'd you get there without me seeing you?'

'It's not my fault you didn't see me,' she says. 'What are you doing up?'

'I was getting a glass of water.' I hold my glass up to show her. 'What were you doing?'

'What is this, an interrogation?' she seethes back.

'Whatever,' I say. 'I'm not in the mood for your games right now. I'm going back to bed.' I turn and make my way back to my room without another word, but not without noticing Beth is no longer in her pyjamas. I also notice she's wearing her sneakers and they're coated in mud. Where has she been?

I push the thought from my mind. There's no way she'll tell me and I'm too tired to try and talk to her about it now.

As I walk into my room exhaustion seeps into my bones. Despite the scare Beth gave me in the hallway, my body feels heavier and only moments after I crawl my way into bed I fall straight to sleep.

WHEN I WAKE in the morning, my room is still dark. It must be early.

I roll over to look at my clock, but the dark red numbers flash '9:00 A.M'. Surprisingly, I've slept in. I sit up in bed and, rubbing my eyes, look out the window. It's incredibly dark outside, but obviously not night.

I heave myself out of bed and drag my feet over to the window to peer up at the sky. The clouds are miserable, grey looking things today. They're almost as dark as the ones I'd seen over the ARC, though strangely devoid of the Lysart purple I'm used to seeing. I can practically feel my mood darken under the oppressive gloom of the day. The blue skies and sunshine are nowhere to be seen.

My nose twitches as it registers the rich smell of frying butter wafting into my room. Visions of Paul's fluffy, warm pancakes appear in my head. In the powerful grip of their smell I am helplessly pulled towards the kitchen, where I find Paul standing over the cook top making breakfast.

I try not to drool as he flips one of the pancakes high in the air. It's hard to contain my excitement over my new favourite meal. Jackson sits eagerly at the kitchen bench waiting for his to be ready.

'Not working today?' I ask Paul, as I take a seat next to Jackson.

'No, sometimes even I get a Sunday off,' he says, looking relieved. He's always so busy with his job for the government; he must really appreciate his time off. 'Are you doing much today?' he asks.

I shake my head. 'Not really. I was thinking of going for a walk.'

He looks meaningfully out the window. 'Don't think you'll have the best weather for walking in today.'

I shrug my shoulders. Bad weather really won't deter me today. I made up my mind last night. I'm going to try and go across the bridge, whether I'm allowed to or not. I can't keep waiting for Sebastian to fall into my lap. At worst they'll turn me away, but maybe, just maybe, they won't and I will find him.

ONCE I'M outside I have to zip my jacket right up. The wind is whipping forcefully around the streets and it cuts coldly into my skin.

There is barely anyone out in the street today and it's unnerving how empty the sidewalk is.

I walk in the direction of the park. From what I saw the other day, the bridge connects to the pathway that winds along the riverbank, so it should be straightforward to make it there.

The park is deserted and I'm hardly surprised after seeing how empty the streets are. It's colder than I've felt on the surface before and, with the wind's icy breath slicing through me, it's not good weather for a visit to the park. It really makes you appreciate the regulated temperature in the ARC. No need for warm, windproof jackets down there.

I easily find my way to the riverbank, thankfully not getting lost this time. Today the river is no longer the majestic, slowly rippling water I'd seen before. The water churns violently, spraying up and over the metal guardrails that line the sidewalk, like it's desperately trying to escape the confines of the riverbank. I stay as far from the edge as possible. My jacket may keep me warm, but it doesn't look like it would fair too well when wet.

The bridge stands down river, closer than I remember. It shouldn't take too long to get there. I can do this. *Easy.* I dig my hands into my jacket pockets for warmth as I set off. With each step I take, my pace quickens and nervous energy tingles at my fingertips. I know I'm onto something, I feel sure of it.

After a while of gazing at the bridge ahead my feet stumble beneath me and I slow to a stand still. The bridge doesn't look any closer. I look over my shoulder at the route I've just walked, before facing the bridge again. It's been nearly ten minutes, and I've come a fair distance. I should be there by now.

'That can't be right.' I shake my head, rejecting the thought. It must just be further than I'd initially assumed.

I wrap my arms across my body, as a strong gust of wind hits me, and I continue walking. It shouldn't take me long now.

The wind gradually gets stronger, howling as it rushes across the river. Pulling my hood up for protection, I lean my body into the wall of air and struggle against it. After another ten minutes, I look up to gauge the distance to the bridge. I'm no closer to it. This time I'm certain.

'Agh!' I throw my hands up in the air, walk up to the nearest tree and slam my fist against it. 'What the hell is going on?' I turn and lean against the tree, staring across the water to the bridge that's no closer, and no further, than before.

Lara had never said it was impossible to go there, she'd just said it wasn't allowed. From what I can see though, you can't get across the bridge even if you want to. I look back up the other direction of the river. This bridge is definitely the only crossing. What do you have to do to cross it?

I bring up the location map on my cuff. As it appears across the glass surface, I do a double take. According to my map I've already walked past the bridge. I look out over the water, back towards the empty space where the bridge is meant to be.

Great! Now my cuff is malfunctioning. I lock the screen angrily. As I do, a water droplet lands on my hand. I look over at the barrier by the river and the water that still thrashes against it. I must be too close. Another water droplet lands on my nose this time. I turn away from the river and start slowly trudging back the way I came.

I will have to convince Lara we should go to the north. There's no way I can go there without her help. Several more water droplets patter on my face. I irritably wipe them away and move closer to the park edge of the pathway.

The droplets begin to become more frequent and much stronger. I realise it's not the river, but the water droplets are plummeting down from directly above me. It's rain. I stand still and look up into the clouds, a sudden excitement gripping me.

I'm in the rain!

I hold my hand out and watch as the water taps lightly on it, before slowly winding its way off of my hand and dripping away. It's mesmerising as it hits the ground and ricochets, each droplet dancing along the pathway. The rain becomes heavier and faster. The light pattering noise as it beats against the ground grows louder and louder.

My initial excitement quickly dissipates as my clothes and hair become sodden and drenched. Even my sneakers become heavy as the water soaks through them. I'd always thought being stuck out in the rain would be romantic or joyous—I guess that's to be expected when you've watched 'Singin' in the Rain' one too many times and never actually been stuck in it.

Now all I can think is that Gene Kelly was obviously a very good actor. After all his singing and dancing in the rain, he probably caught a cold, which is the last thing I want if I'm to avoid ending up in that hospital in the west.

This isn't what I expected at all. My body begins to shiver as the wind bites into my cold wet skin. I pull my arms against my chest and, tucking my head down, I begin my long, miserable journey back to the apartment, my feet squelching against the pavement with every sloshing step.

I may have to convince Lara we need to go over the bridge, but there's no way I'm telling her about this attempt.

CHAPTER TEN

'What are you doing tonight?' Lara asks me, before taking a large bite of her sandwich.

The question makes me sad in a way. I already know she's not about to suggest a trip to North Hope, I'm still a long way off convincing her *that's* a good idea. She won't do anything until we talk to the elusive M.

'Not a lot,' I answer. I had considered going down to look at the bridge again after school, but that's starting to get weird. I've gone and stared aimlessly at it from the riverbank several times this week. I'm still no closer to finding a way over, and swimming across the river is definitely out, considering I've never stood in anything deeper than an inch of water—I should really stop contemplating that as an option.

She looks at the twins, who are deep in conversation across the other side of the table, before saying, 'Don't make any plans. I think you need to let your hair down, relax a little bit. You've been so concerned about Sebastian. We should go and show you what being on the surface is all about.'

'We should?' I ask, trying to keep my disinterest from my voice. This hardly seems the time to be letting my hair down.

Lara doesn't notice my lack of enthusiasm and her head bobs up and down excitedly in response. I have no idea what she wants to do tonight. What do people even do up here for fun? Maybe she's trying to rope me in to a cinema night like the ones we had back in the ARC? It's been ages since I've seen a movie.

I take a long drink from my glass of water and then place it back on the table. 'What will we be doing?' I ask.

'Let's just say it's going to be a surprise. A good one! Just trust me, you will have a blast.'

'I dunno if Cathy will be happy with me going out at night,' I worry.

'Leave Cathy to me,' she says.

'I'm still not sure...'

'If I tell you it'll help us find Sebastian, would that change your mind?'

I glare at her. She's seriously taking advantage of my weaknesses right now.

'Thought so,' she says, with a smile.

'Will it really help us find him?'

'You'll see.'

The bell rings and Lara jumps up from the table. She looks more excited about tonight than I've ever seen her before. It must be contagious because I begin to feel really excited too.

'I have a few things to do after school, so I'll meet you at yours a bit later,' she says, before dashing off ahead of me to class. I take my time gathering my things. Then I leave the cafeteria, walking as slowly as possible, steeling myself to face another session of special studies.

When I enter the classroom it's much the same as last week. The students are seated wherever they feel most comfortable, and they all have their eyes shut as they meditate.

I take the same seat as I had the previous week and take out my tablet. If I have to come to a class there's no point in me being at, I may as well get some work done for my other subjects.

Mr. Kale walks in and, without saying a word, puts his stuff at his desk before sitting on the floor and taking one of the student's hands. As the minutes run by I begin to feel unnerved by the class. No one talks, and Mr. Kale just sits next to different students meditating with them—at least I think that's what they're doing. I look around at the other students silently sitting there. Is this really what they do every lesson?

I find my eyes are continually drawn back to Mr. Kale. I want to know what else he saw when he took my hands last week. I begin to consider asking him to do another reading.

I start tapping my stylus pen against the desk. I can't risk him knowing I'm normal. What would they even do with me if they found out? I wish I could ask someone what would happen without revealing the truth about myself.

I look down at my screen and try to concentrate on my maths homework. I've been doodling in the margins all class, so there's a series of shapes and squiggles surrounding my equations.

'Elle?' I gasp and jump in my seat. Mr. Kale stands right over me, his face thoroughly disapproving. I hadn't even heard him walk over.

He gently takes a hold of my stylus, effectively stopping my tapping, and then tugs it out of my fingers, placing it flat on the table. I look around guiltily. I'd forgotten people were trying to concentrate.

He nods his head over to the door and I follow him outside. He stops just outside the classroom door and looks off into the distance, thoughtful.

'I need you to focus in this class,' he says. 'I know it must be difficult, given your lack of talent, to stay motivated, but you *need* to try.' He turns and stares into my eyes, searching, as if hoping I'll miraculously change.

'I'm sorry Mr. Kale, I understand and will try harder in the future.'

'Please see that you do. It's *important*,' he stresses.

'I will.'

I turn to walk back into class, but he stops me.

'Elle, if your test was wrong and your talent score is a one, which I suspect it is, you're in the wrong area of the city. If I don't see a vast improvement I won't have any choice but to notify the recruiters.'

'What? I don't understand.'

'Everyone with a talent score of one is sent to West Hope. I don't want to send you there but, if a recruiter comes, I won't have any choice in the matter. They are trained to read your talent level and I have no influence over them. I can give you some time to try and improve before I notify them, but if nothing changes...'

'I'll be sent away,' I finish.

His forehead creases and he looks at me, concerned. 'Elle, my door is always open, so you can come chat to me if you ever need to, or you can take on extra lessons if you like.'

I look away, unable to meet his eyes. I will be sent to the west no matter how hard I try or how many extra lessons I take. I am doomed and there's nothing I can do about it. The only thing I can hope for is more time here in East Hope to finish what I started.

'How long do I have?'

'Maybe a few weeks,' he says.

Will that be long enough to find Sebastian? It doesn't seem like nearly enough time. 'I would appreciate as much time as you can give me. I don't want to be sent away.'

'I will try my best, but like I said, if the recruiters come it's no longer up to me.' He pats me on the shoulder and goes to return to the classroom.

'Mr. Kale?' I say, catching his arm. 'Last week, when you read me, you said I was struggling with the loss of my friend. Then you went on to say they were close by. I just wanted to know if you knew any details about where they might be?'

'I never get details like that from what I see,' he explains. 'I get impressions, feelings. I can tell you your friend is here in Hope. But as to where exactly, I don't know.'

'Oh,' I respond.

'I'm sorry Elle. I could tell you both were close. I wish I could be more helpful.' He pushes his glasses up his nose and looks at me, sympathetically. It really seems like he wants to help.

'No, that's okay. I just figured it was worth asking.'

I watch him return to the classroom and as he disappears through the door, I slump down onto the ground, cradling my knees in my arms.

What am I going to do? I'm running out of time.

CHAPTER ELEVEN

everal hours after school finishes for the day, I stand in my room waiting for Lara to arrive. I'd seen her briefly as I'd left school and the only clue she'd given me about tonight was that I absolutely had to dress up. I drag the clothes hangers in my wardrobe back and forth, unable to concentrate on the task at hand. All I can focus on is the fact my life is about to be uprooted again, and I only have a few weeks left in the east.

A million questions tumble through my mind, but the most concerning one is: will I end up sick like the people I saw in the west?

I try to ignore the worry gnawing away at me on the inside and look down at the jeans and t-shirt I'm wearing. Cathy and I had only shopped for the basics when I first arrived, so my wardrobe selection is limited to say the least. I'd been going for comfort when we'd been shopping. I'd never even considered I might need something dressier.

I start rummaging through my drawers trying to find another outfit, but instead of an outfit for tonight all I come across are my greys. I haven't thought about them since arriving here really, but a sense of warmth rushes through me as I pick them up. They feel comforting, so familiar. As I take them out to have a closer look, something falls out of the pocket of the pants.

I bend down and pick up the crinkled ball of paper. I smooth it out carefully. It's the picture Dr. Wilson gave me of his grandson, Aiden, with a message for him, should I find him up here.

I turn the picture over and look at the symbol the doctor drew on the back, slowly tracing my finger over it. I frown as it moves over the crinkles that run through the unusual design. I'd been so angry when I'd carelessly balled it up this way. I thought I'd lost my only way out and blamed Dr. Wilson for it. I'd been wrong to so quickly accuse him though. I was the reckless one, and if anyone was to blame for almost sabotaging my escape, it was myself.

I flip it over to look at Aiden. He has such a kind looking face, and I'm surprised I don't recognise him from the ARC. If only I could help. I'm struggling to find my own friend up here, how can I hope to find him too?

There's a knock at the door and I quickly fold the picture over and put it in my pocket. As the door swings open and Lara bounds in, I put a smile on my face. Tonight, I am determined to try and forget about the picture in my pocket and my imminent departure to the west.

'Heya,' Lara chirps.

'I didn't realise you were here. Did you even ring the doorbell?' I ask.

'Oh, I arrived at the same time as Mr. Mason,' she responds. 'I asked him and he said tonight should be fine. We're all sorted to go.'

'Did you tell him what we're doing?' I ask, curious.

'He thinks we're having a sleepover at mine.'

'We are?' A sleepover doesn't sound too bad. Although I don't know why she expects me to dress up.

'Nope,' she responds. 'Technically you will be sleeping at mine. But that's not what we're doing.' Her lips are pursed mischievously. 'This way we can be out as late as we want.'

'Your parents don't mind?' I ask.

'Nah, it's just my older sister and I up here and she's pretty lax about what I do.' She looks me up and down. 'You will need to wear something slightly nicer than that though,' she says, looking disapprovingly at my standard blue jeans.

'I don't have much else.' Even though I trawled through my wardrobe several times there was nothing appropriate. Lara eyes my wardrobe suspiciously. '*Really,*' I stress.

'Hmm. I'm sure I'll have something that'll work,' she says.

I pack my sleepwear into a small bag and sling it over my shoulder. As we exit into the hallway, I nearly have a head-on collision with Beth.

'Hey Beth,' Lara says, sweetly. Beth raises one eyebrow in return.

'Where are you guys going?' she asks.

'The loft,' Lara replies.

'Really? I'm not sure that's Elle's kind of place.' Her eyes flick over to me as she says this and there's the smallest hint of concern in them.

'I guess we're going to find out,' I say, firmly ending the conversation. I grab Lara's arm and tug her away. 'Bye Beth.'

Once we're out of the hallway, and no longer in Beth's firing line, I let go of Lara's arm and follow her to the front door. I feel a sudden rush of uneasiness though as I replay the conversation with Beth in my mind. Since when has she given a damn about what I do?

By the time we arrive at Lara's apartment I feel quite certain she's about to burst with excitement over whatever she has planned. Her apartment is similar to the Mason's but, because it's smaller and on a lower floor, the views aren't quite as impressive.

'Hey Jess,' Lara says, as we walk into the lounge room. 'This is Elle.'

A girl maybe a few years older than us sits on the couch. She looks very similar to Lara but her eyes are more hazel coloured than brown. 'It's nice to meet you Elle,' she says, formally.

'You too,' I reply.

She sounds so mature. It's hard to believe she's only in her early twenties. I definitely get that 'old-soul' impression with her.

'Jess isn't coming tonight?' I ask, as we walk to Lara's room. I ask the question half because I'm interested in knowing and half because I'm hoping Lara tells me what we're doing.

'No!' she scoffs. 'She's pretty reserved. Would probably prefer staying in reading a book or watching TV.'

'So the place we're going is somewhere reserved people wouldn't want to go?'

Lara gives me a knowing smile at my question. 'You don't think I'll give the game away that easy?' she laughs.

She opens the door to her bedroom and I follow her in. 'Was Jess here when you arrived?' I ask.

'Yeah. It was so strange coming up here last year and finding her after being apart for so long.'

'And are both of your parents still in the ARC?'

'Yes.' Glancing away from me her eyes fixate on the wardrobe. 'Let's go through my clothes and see if we can find something appropriate for you to wear,' she says, changing the subject quickly. I follow her over to the wardrobe and she begins flicking coat hangers of clothes across the rack.

'Are you going to tell me what this place is yet?'

She smiles into her wardrobe. 'Nope. I told you, it's a surprise.' I hope her idea of a surprise isn't something crazy or dangerous. The flicker of concern I'd seen in Beth's eyes comes back to me. Surely Lara wouldn't take me somewhere risky?

'It will be fine. Stop worrying,' Lara says, sensing my apprehension. 'What do you think of this one?' she asks, holding up a black, scoop neck dress.

'It's very short...' I point out. She rolls her eyes and passes me the dress.

'Just try it on. You'll look amazing in it.'

Once I have it on I stand in front of the mirror. The material clings to my body and, as I thought when I first saw the dress, it is extremely short. The only pro is that it has long sleeves, which should at least keep my arms warm tonight.

'I'm not sure,' I say, attempting to tug the bottom of the dress down lower.

'You look hot. Stop stressing. You'll fit right in,' I turn to Lara who's also changed. She's wearing a dark blue low cut top with an even shorter leather skirt.

After an hour spent applying makeup, taming my hair, wedging my feet into heels I can barely walk in and a lot more coaxing from Lara, we both stand in front of the mirror. I can barely recognise myself in my new outfit. Lara's applied my makeup heavily; it makes me look slightly edgy. I definitely look older than I've ever looked before. I wobble slightly in the heels as I take a step forward. I will kill myself in these things tonight.

'I don't think I want to go,' I tell her, as I look myself up and down.

'You look fine,' she says.

'No, I don't. This isn't me, I don't think I should come.'

Lara watches me carefully, almost as if weighing my mood. 'You need to come. I got a message from Josh. He said M will be at the loft tonight and is willing to meet with us.'

'He is? Why didn't you tell me sooner?'

'I didn't want to get your hopes up if he wasn't there,' she says. 'The outfit is necessary if you want to fit in.'

I look back at myself in the mirror. I really don't like what I see there, but it sounds like I don't have a choice if I want to meet M. 'Well then, let's go.'

When we get outside, an icy breeze blows right through me. I huddle my arms closely around my body. I'm so cold I can almost hear my teeth chattering.

'How far is it?' I ask.

'Not far,' Lara responds. She doesn't even look cold, but given her fast pace of walking she must be just as keen to get back inside as I am. I stumble awkwardly in the heels as I try to keep up with her.

The further we walk, the quieter it becomes around us. I've never ventured from the main streets in the east, so I'm surprised to find how different it is in the back blocks. There's barely anyone else on the sidewalk and the street lamps that work become few and far between.

There's garbage in the gutter and the walls of the buildings we pass are covered in the bright, colourful tags of what must be Hope's dedicated group of graffiti artists. This whole area is neglected and too quiet to feel safe. I'm beginning to agree with Beth—wherever we're going, this really isn't my kind of thing.

We arrive out front of a rundown apartment building and Lara walks up the steps to the front door. She turns, noticing I haven't followed.

'Are we really going in there?' I ask, looking up at the broken windows and dark, grimy walls.

'Yep. Come on.' I stare at her for a moment, uncertain. It's the kind of place you'd expect to enter and never walk back out of again.

'C'mon,' she urges, rubbing her arms.

'Alright,' I mutter. Whatever is inside can't be worse than standing out here in the freezing cold.

The inside is as rundown as the outside—worse even. Old, dirty wallpaper dangles from the walls, and a light bulb hangs precariously by its exposed wiring, from a ceiling that looks close to collapse.

'Are you sure we've got the right place?' I ask. Surely we're not meeting M here. Lara merely smiles in response. She walks over to a rusty looking elevator, built into the far wall of the entrance foyer, and presses the button.

'Yes I'm sure. We're going up!' she says. I automatically look around for the stairs, but Lara only laughs, assuming I'm joking when I suggest we use them instead.

When the lift arrives, Lara pulls open the door and pushes aside the inner metal wire gate. I edge my way into the lift after her. She giggles as she sees me bounce lightly on the floor, attempting to test that the thing is still connected.

She presses the button for the top floor and I suck in a quick breath and hold it there as we ascend. I've been better with lifts lately, but I'm still not a huge fan.

'Nearly there,' she says. Her anticipation is contagious and I can feel it beginning to build inside me as well.

When the lift stops again, and she pushes open the door, I am hit by a wall of sound. People are crammed into the hallway in front of us. They are talking and laughing loudly, but that's nothing compared to the overpowering blast of music blaring from somewhere down the other end of the building.

The music is so loud I can feel the vibrations of it shaking the floor beneath my feet. Little flakes of plaster, which have found their way off the decaying walls and onto the floor of the lift, bounce up and down in time to the heavy beat.

We edge our way through the crowd and head towards the noise. I look around curiously, through the open doorways we pass, and at the kinds of people we walk by. None of them indicate what exactly this place is though. Eventually we reach a doorway that is blocked by a large man dressed all in black.

'Hey Daz,' Lara says to him, surprising me. She knows this guy?

'Hey Lara,' he replies.

'Have you seen M tonight?'

'He was in earlier, but I haven't seen him in a while. Maybe check by the bar,' he suggests.

'Okay, thanks.'

'Don't get into too much trouble in there,' Daz warns. Lara winks at him and he stands back to let us past.

She grabs my hand and pulls me along behind her, winding and weaving with ease between the people packed into the corridor. We're just getting to another doorway when I stumble over a loose floorboard. Hobbling behind Lara with my head down, I try to slip one of my feet back into the shoe properly. The things I'd do for some real shoes right now.

When I manage to regain my footing, I look up and do a double take. I'm no longer in the crowded hallway, but in a massive room filled with people dancing.

It's derelict in here, like the rest of the building, but in the darkness with the pulsing coloured lights, it doesn't look so bad. There's the distinct smell of sweat and smoke though, and I cough to clear my throat.

'The loft is a party?' I shout out to Lara over the music.

'Not just *a* party. It's *the* party,' she calls back. 'It's a secret and constantly changes location. There are so many of these abandoned buildings in the city from before, they have a wealth of options and pretty much never get caught.'

'Get caught?' I panic.

'Don't stress, it will be fine. Let's just focus on finding M.'

CHAPTER TWELVE

ara isn't even slightly daunted by the loft party and is quick to drag me straight into the thick of it. Once we're inside, she makes a beeline for the back of the room, where there are several guys standing behind a long bar pouring drinks.

Lara stands on her tiptoes and leans over the bar towards one of the guys behind. 'Hey, have you seen M?' she yells to him.

'Haven't seen him in a while, but I'm sure he's around,' he yells back to her.

'If you see him, will you let him know Lara is looking for him?'

'Will do,' he responds, grinning at her. 'Have a drink while you wait,' he says, lining up four short glasses on the bench and filling them each with a clear liquid, before pushing them towards us.

Lara passes me two and I look down at them, then back up at her, not sure what to do. She is two steps ahead as she throws her head back and drinks the small glass of liquid all at once, then the other one. She looks at me expectantly.

'I don't know if this is a good idea,' I say.

'Don't be silly. You'll be fine,' she says. 'Besides, it'd be rude not to.' She's so certain it's okay, and I don't think she'd ever put me in danger. In fact, she's spent the last week trying to keep me out of it. Plus, she did just have the drink herself.

'C'mon Elle,' she says, laughing. I take my cue from her and toss the drink down my throat. The hot liquid burns and I cough uncomfortably.

'What was in that?'

'And the other one,' she chants, happily ignoring my obvious disgust. Still coughing, I pass the full glass back to her.

She laughs at the pained look on my face, downs my discarded drink and grabs a tall glass filled with a bright pink concoction.

'I think you'll like this a lot better,' she says. It does look more appealing, but I'm not certain I trust the drink. She takes a sip and then offers me a taste.

'Just try some...' she pleads.

I take a cautious sip of the drink and am pleasantly surprised. It's fruity and cold, but tasty and I definitely prefer this to the other one.

'See!' she exclaims, when I don't scrunch my face up, repulsed.

I roll my eyes and pass the drink back to her. 'Should we look for M?' I ask, peering at the men nearby.

'No, if he knows we're looking for him, he'll be the one to come find us. C'mon!' Before I can respond, she grabs my arm and drags me into the crowd of people. Again she glides easily between them. I, on the other hand, bump, slam and trip into everyone I pass. 'Excuse me,' will be my official phrase of the night.

Lara stops when she finds a gap and begins dancing. I cross my arms over my chest and look around us. 'Will M be able to find us here?'

'Stop worrying, he probably won't be able to talk until this all dies down, and we need to look like we fit in. We may as well have a little fun while we wait.'

I sigh and begin to shuffle awkwardly beside her, trying to avoid knocking into anyone else. Once we've been dancing for a while I begin to feel more at ease. This isn't so bad.

'How amazing is this?' Lara yells to me over the music. I give her two thumbs up, causing her to laugh. I guess giving the thumbs up is stupid both above and below ground.

As we continue to dance I begin to feel lightheaded. I shake my head, trying to clear it. What was in that drink?

'Hey! Watch it!' Lara yells at some guy who's just barrelled into her. She stares him down staggering unsteadily on her feet.

'You watch it!' he yells back, shoving her roughly.

'Did you just push her?' Another guy asks, pointing his finger at the first guy's head. Without waiting for a response his fist flies through the air, connecting with a loud *thud* against the guy's cheek.

The fight escalates rapidly when several other people get involved, throwing punches and shoving each other. I would normally feel worried or apprehensive, or at the very least scared, but instead I can feel anger building inside of me. Who do these people think they are?

I'm shoved from behind and am propelled into one of the brawling men. His hulk-like muscular form turns, his shoulders shuddering with anger. His mad-glinting eyes search for his new opponent, and look down on me. A terrifying look of satisfaction overcomes him.

'You want a piece of me sweetheart?' he jeers. Instead of cowering, like any sane person would, I'm furious that he thinks he can have a go at me.

'Bring it!' I yell, taking a step towards him and thumping my fists against my chest. His lip curls cruelly at the side as he clenches his fist and pulls his thickly muscled arm backwards. I close my eyes as the fist shoots towards my face.

I feel impact, but it's not the impact I had been expecting. Instead of my face being pummelled, I'm thrown sideways. I land heavily on the floor, a dead weight landing on top of me. All the air rushes out of my lungs and I struggle to breathe.

I cough and open my eyes to find Lara on top of me, her face the picture of worry and concern.

'Oh God, I'm so sorry Elle. Are you okay?' she asks. I shake my head trying to clear the fog that sits there.

'I think so,' I reply. Feeling dazed, I look up and the fighting has stopped. People dance around us calmly, and given the way they tranquilly sway, you'd swear they were in a trance.

I ease myself back up off the floor and look around. It's like the brawl had never happened. I shake my head again to clear the fog. Surely I didn't imagine it? I rub the sides of my tender battered body; the fall had been so painful, I'm certain I hadn't imagined that.

'What happened?' I ask Lara, whose face has turned ghostly pale. She glances over at the other people dancing then back at me.

'Come with me,' she says, tugging my sleeve and dragging me towards the bar, which is a bit quieter. When we reach the corner of the room she turns back to me, tears welling at the corners of her eyes.

'It's all my fault,' she says. 'I did this!' She looks over my shoulder with concern; like she's worried the brawl will start all over again.

'Lara, you can't blame yourself for that ass knocking into you. If it's anyone's fault, it's his.'

She shakes her head violently. 'No, you don't understand, it's *my* fault.' She leans towards me, putting her mouth close to my ear. 'I'm talented,' she whispers. It's said so quietly I nearly don't catch her words at all.

Her face is filled with worry when she pulls back from my ear. She watches me, not saying a word, waiting for my reaction.

'You're talented?' I repeat, confirming what she's said.

She nods her head, looking nervous about how I will respond. Talented or not, she can't have possibly wanted this to happen. 'What did you do exactly?'

She looks over my shoulder again before she talks. 'I can feel and affect other people's emotions,' she says, quietly. 'I got angry when that guy shoved me, and I'd had a few drinks, so I lost control. Everyone around me could feel my anger, and I in turn felt theirs, which only made it worse. It was like everyone was fuelling each other in a bad, *bad* chain reaction. It took me a while to realise it was even my fault, I'm just glad I realised before something bad happened to you.'

I look at her with disbelief. 'How did you do that?'

'I don't know how it works,' she says. 'Dammit though, I've been doing so well with it.' Her face frowns with frustration.

Someone brushes past me and I look behind me to find even more people flowing into the small space. I'm starting to feel stifled with all these people around. Not to mention that I can practically feel the bruises beginning to form on me from my fall. I'll have plenty of time to ask Lara questions about her talent tomorrow. For now, we need to get out of here.

'We should go home,' I suggest, but Lara shakes her head at me.

'No,' she says, regaining her composure. 'We haven't seen M yet and we may not get another chance like this for weeks. I'm fine now, I swear.'

I'm not convinced it's a good idea, but I don't have much of a choice. I don't have long left in East Hope to wait for another chance. Before I can answer she's dragging me towards the bar.

'Any sign of M?' she asks the bartender again.

'Nope. Sorry love,' he says, pushing more drinks towards her.

'Drink,' she orders, handing me two of the small glasses.

'No, I don't like those.' I attempt to hand them back, but she refuses.

'It will make you feel better. Trust me.' I look her in the eyes and she seems convinced it will help.

'Okay,' I grumble, finishing both the drinks. I cough and splutter after each one. 'Those are horrible. You know that, right?'

She laughs as I screw my face up. 'Come on. Let's try dancing again.'

I try to tell her it's a bad idea, but she won't listen and drags me back onto the dance floor.

There's even less space than before as we try to dance. I'm constantly touching or being touched by other people. I can feel the sweat from some guy's back on my arm and the gyrations of some girl pushing herself up against another guy.

As we continue to dance, more and more people cram their way onto the dance floor. My thoughts become muddled and I find it harder to stay steady in my heels.

'What was in those drinks?' I ask Lara.

'Some of the loft party's famous moonshine.'

I shake my head, trying to think clearly. 'Alcohol right?'

She looks at me confused and then bursts out laughing. 'You didn't realise there was alcohol in those?'

'I did, I'm not an idiot, I just didn't realise it would be so strong,' I say, as I stumble backwards into the girl behind me. Lara continues laughing, obviously finding this hilarious.

The dizziness begins to get worse. I keep trying to clear my mind and think straight, but the murkiness only gets more intense. How can this M guy help me if I'm too intoxicated to help myself?

A guy bumps me from behind and I roll in my heels as I try to maintain my balance. I turn, looking for some space where I'll be safe from being knocked, but the crowd is closing in around us. I tug at the top of my dress, trying to let some cool air in. It's getting really hot in here.

I am enclosed by bodies. I can feel my chest constricting. I need to get out of here *now*.

'I need some space,' I call to Lara. 'I'm going back to the bar.'

'Want me to come?' Lara asks. She's dancing with a guy I recognise from school, so I shake my head.

'I'm okay,' I mumble, lurching away from her towards the edge of the crowd.

I'm almost there when I notice a group of people have stopped dancing in the middle of the dance floor. Their faces appear worried and several of them are pointing over towards the entranceway. I stop and look back around the room. Everything looks normal—well as normal as I expect some secret rooftop dance party can be. Wait, did I just see Beth?

I step up onto my tiptoes to try and get a better look, but the room plunges into darkness and the thudding beat of the music disappears. For just one second there is complete and utter silence. For a moment it's as though I'm the only person here. My ears ring and there is a stillness to the room.

'Recruiters!' A male voice bellows. All at once people start screaming.

In the darkness bodies slam into me in rapid succession as people begin to try and make their way towards the exit.

I'm blindly tossed around as I get pushed and shoved in every direction.

I have no idea what is happening so I try to make my way back to where I'd last seen Lara.

'Lara?' I attempt to yell her name over the deafening screams that rip through the crowd.

'Lara!' I call her name again, but it's useless. I can barely hear myself yelling, so she's got no chance of hearing me. I bring her username up on my cuff and attempt to comm her, but for some reason the signal is blocked and I can't get through.

I allow myself to get pulled along with the rushing crowd, but I am still thrown back and forth as people violently whip past me in their frenzy to escape. Someone knocks past my shoulder hard and I grab it as I scream out in pain.

Still gripping my shoulder, the crowd surges and I become squashed between two men. I cry out for them to stop. I can't breathe, my ribs feel like they're being crushed.

The crowd surges backwards and I'm freed from between the two men. I clamber away from them, desperate to escape.

A light flashes in my eyes, blinding me momentarily, before moving on. There must be a dozen beams of light shining around the room. I don't want to be afraid, but I have no idea what's going on, why people are running scared. I thought most people wanted to be recruited?

I am cold and shaky as I struggle to stay standing. Every time someone shoves me I roll in my heels and fall towards the floor. If it weren't for the people I've been wedged between, I would've been road kill as soon as this started.

I catch a glimpse of the exit in the distance before being pulled down again by the bodies crowded around me. It's so close now, and the crowd of people continue to push me towards it.

I'm almost at the door when the people around me surge forward again and I'm flung to the floor. There's a dull thud as my head cracks against the hard wooden surface.

I try to open my eyes but the whole floor feels like it's rocking. I want to roll over but as soon as I move I feel sick—a queasy kind of sickness, where I'm no longer certain dinner is safely settled in my stomach. I close my eyes, but the world still spins beneath me. I don't like this feeling at all.

'Elle?' a man's voice asks me. I don't respond. I'm not certain I can form the words. All I want to do is sleep.

'Elle!' the voice yells, louder this time. Someone grabs my shoulders and pulls me up into a sitting position. My head rolls down like a rag doll's.

'Elle's not here right now,' I mumble.

An arm wraps around my shoulders and I lean in, resting my head in the crook of their arm against their shoulder. This is such a nice place and it smells so good. *I think I'd like to sleep here,* I muse. Snuggling into the crook, I feel safe and warm. The world quickly falls away and I'm peaceful in total oblivion.

CHAPTER THIRTEEN

Bright, white, light. Even with my eyelids shut I can feel the intensity of the light searing through my lids to my eyes. I groan out loud. *It's just too bright.* I feel for the edge of my quilt cover and throw it over my head.

Much better.

But slowly, as my eyes adjust to the darkness, I begin to notice other feelings. My head is pounding. My mouth is dry. My body feels like it's rocking, even though I know I'm still.

A man laughs and I sit bolt upright in bed. Opening my eyes, it takes me a few moments to register where I am and the fact this is not my bed.

The laughter sounds again and looking towards the door I find Hunter lounging against the doorway.

'Morning,' he says.

'Where am I? What happened?' I look around wildly, trying to determine my location. Hunter comes and sits at the end of the bed, looking thoroughly amused by my reaction.

'You're at my place,' he explains, passing me a glass of water.

'What?' I look at the room and see it properly for the first time.

I'm sitting in the middle of a large double bed with crisp white sheets. There are wooden floors and white walls with a large window across one of them. It's incredibly nice.

'You like it?' he asks.

'No,' I respond, defensively, causing him to laugh again.

'Drink up.' He nods at the glass of water, which I gulp down.

'How did I get here?' I ask, placing the glass down on the bedside table.

'I found you passed out on the floor at the loft last night. I had no idea who you were with and you would've been trampled if I just left you there, so I brought you back here.'

'Oh,' I mutter, embarrassed. 'Thank you for helping me.' I can't believe I'm thanking this guy. In what world did I ever expect that to happen?

'It was no problem. To be honest I was surprised to see you there. I didn't expect the loft to be your kind of scene,' he mocks.

'It's not. I had no idea where Lara was taking me and I've never had alcohol before, which probably didn't help. What happened there?'

'There was a recruiters raid.'

'But I thought people wanted to be recruited?'

Hunter laughs. 'Most people do. But those recruiters weren't there for that last night. They came to break up the party.'

'Oh,' I reply, for lack of a better response. I still can't believe last night happened. If we hadn't been meeting M I never would've stayed at a place like that. I slump back in the bed as I realise I missed my chance to talk to him.

'You okay?'

I ignore his question, instead asking, 'Do *you* go there often?'

'Often enough. It's a good place to pick up girls,' he says. An emotion I can't quite label prickles inside of me as he says that. He's a flirt and a tease; it makes sense for him to frequent places like the loft.

'Although normally they don't involve such heavy lifting,' he says, winking.

'Oh,' I respond, uncertain what he means. 'Oh!' I exclaim as realisation dawns. My cheeks flush quickly as I realise he had to carry me home.

Did he really carry me the whole way here? I size up the muscles on his arms. They're impressive enough that I'm sure he had no problems carrying me, but even so, I hope it wasn't far. I feel my cheeks grow warmer as I realise I've been staring at his biceps just a few seconds too long. I quickly look away.

'Did you see Lara at the loft?' I ask, hoping she's okay.

'No, but I'm sure she's fine. She's extremely capable of looking after herself.' I hope so. She'd drunk just as much as me, more even, and with everything that happened with the recruiters...

'Do you want to comm her?' he asks.

'Yeah. Good idea.'

I look down at my CommuCuff and notice I'm wearing a baggy basketball top I'm one hundred per cent certain I wasn't wearing last night. I don't remember changing...

'Ah Hunter? Where are my clothes?' I ask, mortified.

He chuckles in response. 'Don't stress, you changed into that yourself. Although I was more than willing to help you.' His lips struggle to suppress a smile. 'Your dress is hanging over the back of the chair.' He nods to the chair over by the window.

'Right. And, um, where did you sleep?'

'You've got lots of questions this morning, haven't you?'

'Hunter?'

'On the couch. You can feel free to comm Lara at any time you know.' Right. Lara. I bring up her username on my cuff and hit connect. I watch the blue light on the screen as it pulses, waiting for her to pick up. Worry starts gnawing at me. Why isn't she picking—

'Hello?' Lara answers, groggily. I feel automatic relief.

'Hey, it's Elle.'

'Oh my god, Elle. Are you okay?'

'I'm fine,' I reassure her. 'Did you get out okay?'

'Yeah, I was totally fine. Where are you? I couldn't find you last night.'

'I'm at Hunter's,' I reply, my eyes flicking up to his face, before quickly looking away.

'Oh, I see how it is. You know, I was worried sick. I waited for you after the raid for ages and tried a million times to comm you, but the signal was blocked. You could've told me if you wanted to leave with him.'

'No, no, no! It was nothing like that. I was pushed over during the raid and I think I hit my head and passed out. Then Hunter found me and, since he didn't know who I was there with, he was kind enough to bring me here.' I can feel his eyes watching me, making me conscious of how much I say to Lara.

'You passed out?' she asks.

'Yeah.'

'Shit, Elle, that's horrible. I hope you're okay.'

'I'm fine,' I reassure her again.

'I feel so bad. I was the one who took us there and you ended up hurt. I can't believe it! On the upside, I guess we'll know to be more careful next time.'

I scoff, but then cover it with a cough. *I'm pretty certain there won't be a next time.*

Lara continues, 'I'm sorry I didn't manage to find M, what with the raid and all—'

'I'll come by your place to get my stuff on the way home,' I say, talking over her and hoping she'll get the hint. Hunter's not even trying to be subtle about listening in.

'Oh yeah. I'll be around all day, so swing by whenever. Have fun with *Hunter*,' she croons.

I can feel myself blushing and I keep my eyes looking determinedly away from him. 'Okay, I'll see you soon. Bye.' I say the words quickly and disconnect our comm without waiting for her response. She's already embarrassed me enough and I'm not willing to see what else she can add to mortify me further.

'What are we going to do for fun then? You weren't much fun last night,' Hunter says.

'I, uh...'

'I'm kidding Elle. I'm making us some breakfast. How about you change and meet me out in the kitchen?'

My tummy growls as he says it and I laugh at it. 'That would be great.'

Squeezing back into the dress from last night is a feat. It feels even shorter in the daylight. The heels are on the floor next to the chair, but my feet are still throbbing from last night, so I decide to leave them off.

I cautiously make my way out into the bright open plan living and kitchen area. The decor is sleek and white, very modern, with huge windows that give the room an airy, light feeling. I look around to see if there's anyone else home but only see Hunter behind the kitchen counter.

'Something smells good,' I say.

'I hope you like eggs.'

'I do.' I take a seat at the counter.

'Why were you looking for M last night?' he asks.

'No idea, I think he's a friend of Lara's. Who else lives here?' I ask, attempting to avoid all talk of M.

'It's just me.'

'You weren't fostered out?'

'I was originally. But I decided to move out on my own.'

'They let you do that?' I ask.

'Not really, but I didn't like living with some strange family and I didn't want to get moved into the East Dorms. There are so many empty apartment buildings, I just decided to pick one and make the most of it.'

'You just moved in?'

'Yep.' He pulls out some toast from the toaster, juggling the hot pieces and tossing them down on a plate.

'Where's your own family?'

'Still in the ARC,' he replies. I'm not surprised; the ARC was filled with torn families, so obviously the same would be true of the surface.

'Voila.' He places the plate in front of me.

'This looks delicious.' It smells even better. He brings his plate around to sit next to me. We both sit in silence as we munch away at our breakfast.

'Who's Sebastian?' he asks. A piece of food gets caught in my throat and I cough uncomfortably, trying to clear it.

'A friend of mine,' I say quickly. I take several deep gulps of water. 'Why?'

'You were just talking about him last night is all.'

'I was?'

'Yeah,' he says. I push my food around my plate, waiting for him to continue, but he doesn't say anything.

'What did I say?' I finally ask.

'Just random things, nonsense mostly.' We go back to eating in silence. He doesn't stop there though. 'Are you looking for him?'

'Yes.'

'I thought you might be.' He nods to himself. The silence has turned uneasy in the room. I quickly heap the last few bites of my breakfast into my mouth.

'I should go. Do you need any help cleaning up?' I ask, as I take my plate into the kitchen. It's taking a lot of effort to act casual and hide the mounting anxiety I feel to leave the apartment. The whole place has become repellent to me and my body craves some fresh air. It's probably just because I've been feeling a bit sick this morning.

'No, I'm happy to do it,' he replies, following me with his own plate.

My shoulders noticeably sag in relief and I quickly move towards the front door. Hunter pulls it back for me.

'I'll see you at school on Monday,' I say, when I get to the entrance.

'Yeah, see you then,' he says, watching me as I leave. It's only when I'm several feet down the corridor that I hear the click of the door shutting behind me.

In my hurry to get out, it's not until I reach the lift that I realise how dingy the hallway is. None of the lights are on, and the only source of light is from a window at the other end of the corridor. The floor is covered with a frayed carpet runner and the walls are dirty, with sections of panelling missing in places. It reminds me of the dilapidated entrance to the building we were in last night. The elevator looks just as old and creaky. I repeatedly push the button to call for the lift.

'C'mon, c'mon,' I grumble under my breath. The lift doesn't come though and I have to take the stairs. Once I'm in the stairwell I begin to relax. I feel foolish for being so desperate to leave Hunter's apartment, especially after everything he did for me last night. By the time I reach the lobby I feel like an absolute idiot.

The lobby is similar to the hallway upstairs in that it's completely run-down. There's even a fallen chandelier by the entranceway. No wonder no one else wants to live here. Hunter's done an amazing job on his place.

'Ouch,' I squeal. I look down and realise I've stepped on some broken glass. I hop backwards on one foot. I've forgotten my heels. *Shit.* I look back towards the stairwell. I really can't be bothered going back up, but there's no way I'm walking home barefoot. How did I manage to get all the way down here without noticing?

When I get back to Hunter's apartment I politely knock on the door. He doesn't answer. I stand and wait for a moment before I knock again.

'Hunter?' I call through the door. Again there's no reply. I look up and down the hallway. Is it darker up here than before? I try the door.

Nervously I twist the doorknob and it turns. I feel bad barging in, but it's creepy in the hallway and I really don't want to wait for him out here. He's probably only doing the dishes anyway.

'Sorry Hunter—' I say as I enter, but I stop abruptly, frozen to the spot. I must have the wrong apartment.

I slowly take a few steps forward. The apartment has the same layout as Hunter's but it's completely neglected, just like the rest of the building. I shake my head. I definitely have the wrong apartment. The windows that I remember letting in streams of light are covered in dust and grime. Long dark shadows cover the room. The shiny modern surfaces I had admired just a few minutes ago look tired and broken. The wooden floors are scratched and cracking and, in one place where I could've sworn a couch sat, the boards have rotted away to leave a massive gaping hole. As I go to leave I spot plates on the kitchen bench. *Our* plates on the kitchen bench. They are the only things in this place that look exactly as I remember.

I turn and creep further into the apartment.

'Hunter?' I call again.

'Elle!' He jumps, spotting me as he walks out of the bathroom from the other side of the kitchen. He's dripping wet and only wearing a towel. He grabs a shirt off one of the chairs and rushes over to me.

I'm officially going crazy. Maybe I'm *really* sick and hallucinating? Or maybe I'm still dreaming? I pinch my arm—*Ouch*. No, definitely not a dream.

'What is this?' I mutter to myself.

'I can explain,' he says, pulling the shirt down over his dripping wet chest. Yeah, I'm definitely in a dream, or maybe I'm being used on some weird episode of Talented?

'Wait, Talented,' I stutter. 'You're talented.'

'Yes,' he replies.

'And you made me see that writing,' I say, slowly.

'Yes.' He looks nervous.

I pause, watching him, allowing the cogs in my brain to slowly turn. 'It was never there. Was it?'

'No,' he says.

'Your perfect apartment was never there?'

'No.'

'How...'

He pulls his hand up through his wet hair, his face troubled. 'I can do things with people's minds...'

I involuntarily take a step back. 'What kind of things?'

'Ah geez Elle...' He looks away from me, searching for the words to explain.

'What kind of things?' I repeat more forcefully. He turns back to me and takes a deep breath before he continues.

'Like reading people's minds,' he says, his eyes looking down to his feet. I take another step back towards the door. 'Like being able to manipulate minds and change what people see.'

'You've read my mind?'

His eyes dart back up to my face. 'Yes,' he breathes.

I look at him with horror and disgust. How dare he? Doesn't he realise it's a total invasion of privacy?

'I know,' he says.

'What?'

'I know it's an invasion of privacy,' he replies.

You're reading my thoughts now? I think. Despite everything I've seen and heard, I'm still unable to comprehend it's even possible.

'Yes.' He looks anxious as he admits this. Like he's uncomfortable confirming the reality of what he can do.

'Could you not?' I reply, folding my arms against my chest.

'Would it make a difference?' There's a sadness to his voice, like he already knows he's condemned.

'Yes!' I exclaim, surprised he even has to ask.

We stand in awkward silence. Neither one of us is sure of what to say. This is all too much.

My stomach plummets. What if he *knows* the truth about me? I look up at him cautiously. Would he tell anyone if he knew? If he doesn't know, I can't risk him finding out. I have to get out of here.

'Elle. Not many people know the extent of what I can do. This is why—it freaks people out,' he says, finally breaking the silence.

'I'm not freaked out,' I retort.

He lifts his eyebrows up at me. 'Really?'

'Maybe a little,' I admit. I sigh as his eyebrows rise higher with disbelief. 'Maybe a lot.'

He turns and begins pacing, his stance rigid and his steps abrupt. He folds his arms over his chest and stares down at the floor.

'Why go to all the effort of showing me a place that doesn't exist?' I ask.

He stops pacing and turns to me, pain evident on his face. 'Because I didn't want you to wake up in this horrible apartment and be scared,' he responds, obviously embarrassed. 'Then when you'd been here for a while I found it was too much to keep holding the illusion. I had to give you a push to leave.'

'You did that?' He nods seriously in response. 'That's why I left so suddenly?'

'Yes.'

'Why aren't you on the northern side of the river then?' I ask.

He takes a moment and considers the question before he replies. 'Because I don't want to be,' he says. 'They got my test wrong and when I started developing this talent I decided to mask it from the recruiters.'

'But why?' I ask.

'Because I refuse to be what this supposedly *perfect* society wants me to be. I was forced to leave my mum. I didn't get a choice. I didn't even get a goodbye. They drugged me when I wouldn't come quietly, then forced me into a new family, a new school, and a whole fucking new life. It's just one more decision I've decided they're not going to make for me.'

'I'm sorry,' I whisper. I know how he feels but, unlike him, I did have a choice.

'I don't need your pity.' We stand in silence. I can almost feel the tension rolling off his skin.

'I should go.' I don't wait for his response. I hurry into his room, pick up my shoes and go to the front door. As I pull it open he comes to stand behind me.

'Elle, you're limping. Are you okay?'

'I'm fine,' I respond, despite the pain in my foot. He doesn't want my pity and I can't stand the idea of his sympathy right now.

Hunter sighs. 'You'll know where you are when you get outside. I live on the same route to school as you.'

'Okay,' I respond, bluntly.

It's not until I'm out on the street that I consider just how careful I will need to be around him now. I can't risk him reading my thoughts and discovering that I am not even talentless, and that I plotted my escape from the ARC.

I hug my arms around my body and sigh loudly. I don't know how to act around him now or if I can believe that he won't read my mind. If there's one thing this has shown me, it's that maybe Sophie was right—he can't be trusted.

CHAPTER FOURTEEN

'Hunter's watching you again...' Sophie says. She nods her head towards one of the tables behind me, but I shrug and focus back down on my food. I become acutely aware of the back of my neck. I can practically feel Hunter's stare boring into it from the other side of the cafeteria.

'You can't ignore him forever,' Lara adds. We haven't spoken since Hunter told me the truth about himself—not for a lack of attempts on his part.

'I can try,' I mutter into my food. I glance up at Lara, who's looking at me disapprovingly.

'What?' I ask, innocently.

'Elle, we get there can be a lot to get used to up here. But *he* can't help his talent. Just as much as you can't help being untalented,' Lara says.

'So...'

'He did the right thing by you. Looked after you when you needed it. He made you see things that weren't there because he didn't want to scare you,' she says, lowering her voice.

I gulp down an oversized chunk of food, which sits uneasily in my stomach. It's getting harder and harder to pretend that I can't accept his talent. I can't risk him finding out about me, but I can't exactly give that explanation to Lara and Sophie. How much longer can I keep this up?

'The problem is that I didn't give him permission to *do* that,' I say, pushing the food around my plate with my fork. 'I don't know how to be friends with someone who can do things I can't, especially when he's happy to use them against me.'

Sophie clears her throat and excuses herself from the table. She directs her words towards Lara and refuses to look at me as she leaves. I've clearly pissed her off with what I've just said.

'I didn't mean her talent, or yours for that matter,' I add, when Lara raises an eyebrow at me. 'I just don't know how to cope with Hunter's talent.'

'I find it hard to believe you struggle so much with his talent and yet you're fine with mine. I could just as easily manipulate you with my talent,' she says, being careful not to let her words carry to the kids who sit at the table next to us.

I think back to the night I'd learnt what Lara could do. Empathy, she'd called it the following day. It had been an accident she'd used it on me that night, and she'd been so upset about what she'd done after.

'Elle?' Lara says, waiting for my response.

'You wouldn't do that on purpose,' I say.

'Wouldn't I?'

'No,' I say, sounding less certain.

'Elle, I'm making you feel unsure as we speak,' Lara whispers.

'Why would you do that?'

'And Sophie uses her talent every time she touches someone, whether she wants to or not.' Which is exactly the reason I've avoided touching her, she's pretty much a human lie detector.

'You need to understand that what we can do is a part of who we are. I use my talent all the time. Sometimes I don't even realise I'm doing it. It's only natural, and that doesn't make me a bad person.'

'But he's using his talent to change things about people they may not want changed. He's reading people's thoughts, whether they want him to or not. He's abusing his talent.' I don't know what else I can say to get her off my back about this, and I can't understand why she feels so strongly about me freezing Hunter out.

Lara stands up and considers me, with a look of concern in her eyes. 'The world is different up here, people are different, and you need to come to terms with that if you want to adjust to living on the surface.'

She doesn't wait for my response. Instead, she turns and strides away, heading for the cafeteria's exit. I call out her name, hoping she'll give me the chance to explain, but she ignores it, disappearing outside.

Lara mustn't think very much of me right now. I as good as told her I couldn't accept talented people, which isn't really true. I can accept people's talents, I just can't risk being near anyone who can find out the truth about me.

I sigh and lay my head down against my arms on the table. I scrunch my eyes up and pray the act will make me disappear.

'Penny for your thoughts?' Hunter asks, from behind me. I try not to jump in surprise. I'd assumed everyone had left the cafeteria by now.

'Go away Hunter,' I grumble back. Like he doesn't already know what I'm thinking. The chair next to me scrapes against the concrete floor. I slowly sit up, opening my eyes.

'Don't pretend you didn't already check what's going on up here.' I drum my fingers against my forehead.

'You asked me not to,' he says, leaning casually back in his chair.

'Right. There's no way I can tell whether you are. So, of course you're respecting my wishes. You are not reading my mind, or making me see things.'

He smiles at me and shakes his head, decidedly ignoring my rant. 'Are you sitting here all afternoon, or are you going to head to class?' he asks.

'I have a free period,' I explain.

'Lucky for you, I do as well.'

Perfect.

I'd done such a good job at avoiding him so far, and now I'm trapped with him for an entire free period. Doesn't he realise I don't want to talk to him?

'Will you tell me what's wrong?' he asks. 'You know, give me an explanation for why, when you see me walking towards you, you turn and run in the other direction?'

'You noticed that?'

'Yeah, I noticed,' he replies.

I look down at my hands. My fingers are tearing at the skin around my nails. I haven't done that bad habit in years. I self-consciously lay them flat on the table, as I try to find the words to describe how I feel. I don't want to hurt him, and I can't tell him the whole truth, but there's no point in even having this discussion if I'm not honest with him. I take a deep breath before I start.

'It scares me,' I begin in a small voice. 'What you can do, I mean. There are things about me I wouldn't want anyone to know. How do I know you're not sifting through my brain for my deepest, darkest secrets? How can I know my thoughts are truly my own when I'm around you?'

'You can't. You just have to trust me.'

I scoff. 'Trust isn't something you can just expect. It needs to be earned.'

'I understand that. I won't use it on you though. I respect that you don't want me fiddling around up there,' he points to my forehead, 'so I won't.'

'Why wouldn't you do it? Lara says it's only natural.'

'Lara's talent is different to mine. I have to actively be trying to hear people's thoughts. Let alone mind manipulation. I can still barely do that.'

'Didn't look like you could barely do it to me,' I say. He was quite capable of making me see an elaborate apartment that wasn't there.

He shrugs. 'You were tired and you'd hit your head. You could barely make a coherent thought, let alone fight against my influence. It makes it a lot easier.' He looks down at his own hands before he continues. 'I guess my motivation was also stronger than the other times I've attempted it.'

'How so?' He looks away from me, over to the kitchen hands clearing away the food from lunch. 'Hunter?'

'I was embarrassed,' he begins. 'I live in a complete shambles of an apartment. It was the last place in the world I would've wanted to take you, but I didn't really have a choice. I wasn't going to just leave you there with those recruiters.

'When I saw you stirring in the morning I began to freak out. I couldn't have you waking up in such a derelict place. I didn't want you to be scared.' He places his head in his hands in frustration.

'I appreciate what you did, really I do, but it doesn't change how I feel.' Or does it? He's done nothing but look out for me since we met. Maybe I'm wrong about him? He seems so genuine in what he's saying. Maybe I've been wrong to think I can't trust him ... he's actually kind of sweet when he's not being so arrogant.

I push my chair back abruptly, the metal whining against the concrete, and stand. I refuse to let myself think these things, to so easily change my mind. He can't know the truth about me, so we can't be friends, that's all there is to this. Without a word I walk outside.

'Elle?' Hunter calls after me. I don't turn back to his voice. Instead, I try clear my mind by concentrating on the fresh, cool breeze that hits me as I leave the building. What is wrong with me?

'Elle!' His hand grabs a hold of my shoulder, wrenching me around. 'What are you doing?'

'I'm getting some air.' I thought he was sweet. I obviously need it.

'So suddenly?'

His words make me pause to search his eyes. My thoughts had so quickly turned to accepting him without the slightest consideration for my real problem with his talent. It wasn't until I was outside again that I could think clearly.

'It was you? Wasn't it?' I say.

'What?'

'I'm not stupid you know.' I shake my shoulder out from under his hand and start to walk away, intending go to my locker, get my bag and go home. I'm completely over today, and I no longer care what the repercussions for missing a lesson are. I've already been doomed to be sent to the west

Two steps out though I get another wave of anger towards him and turn to him. I'm not letting him get away with manipulating me that easily.

'You know that was a *really* low blow,' I say. 'How can you ever expect me to trust you, when you can't even keep your word in the short term?'

'What are you talking about?' he asks, looking more frustrated than guilty.

'You know,' I say firmly, folding my arms across my chest.

'No I don't,' he replies steadily. 'Your little outburst is enough to make me want to read your mind though. Seriously!' he exclaims, throwing his hands in the air.

'You really have no idea?' I ask. He looks confused and pretty annoyed by my outburst. If he'd actually manipulated my thoughts he'd probably laugh and fess up to it, rather than react the way he has.

'No,' he replies.

I back away from him. *Oh shit.* I've made a complete idiot out of myself.

He looks at me, still confused, but then his eyes light up. 'You think I manipulated you,' he accuses.

'No!' I take several steps back further.

'No, you said I can't keep my word.'

'I didn't mean...'

'You really think I'd manipulate you to accept me?' he asks, hurt clear on his face.

'No,' I reply, feeling like an absolute idiot for throwing around false accusations. Especially when it's clear how much it's hurt him. 'I'm really sorry. I'm just confused.'

He looks into my eyes. Seeing what's there his shoulders relax slightly and the hurt lessens on his face.

'I barely know you and it's hard to know who you can trust up here.' I trust him about as far as I could throw him, but I can't exactly say that.

He begins to pace back and forth. 'What if I could do something to earn your trust?' he asks.

'Like what?' I say, my curiosity piqued.

'Like helping you find your friend Sebastian.'

'You'd do that?'

'If it would mean you'd trust me.'

'But why? Why does gaining my trust even matter?' I ask.

He looks at me for a moment before turning away. 'When you first got here I had a glimpse into your mind and straight away I knew I wanted to be your friend. You talk of gaining trust, and I know better than most how hard it can be to trust people. There are only a handful of people I trust up here, and you're one of them, so I guess that's why I want you to trust me so bad.'

I shuffle my feet uncomfortably.

He sighs and turns back. 'Will you please just let me help you?' he asks. 'I may be one of the few people here who can.'

I'm not in any position to turn down offers for help at this point, and maybe, with Hunter's aid, I'll actually get closer to finding Sebastian? Part of me wants to give him the chance to gain my trust, and I'm about 90% certain that's all me.

'Yes,' I respond. 'Thank you.' We stand in silence for a moment before Hunter speaks up.

'So, we're friends now, you've slept in my bed, we've got ourselves a mission to accomplish and I'm pretty sure I caught you eyeing me up earlier. What's the next step in our relationship?' he jokes.

I roll my eyes and laugh despite myself. 'You're terrible. You are aware of that, right?'

'Completely.' He throws his arm over my shoulder. 'C'mon, let's get you to your next class. If we stand out here any longer someone might catch you drooling over me again,' he laughs.

'You wish,' I say.

'You're the one doing the drooling.'

'Stop it!' I plead.

He chuckles under his breath. As we walk towards the next class I watch him out of the corner of my eye. It's nice to finally understand why he wants me to trust him. I'll still have to be careful of my thoughts when I'm around him though.

Hunter holds out his hand, stopping me abruptly.

'Don't move.'

'What's wrong?' I ask, looking up at him. A hard look of concentration has come over his face. 'Hunter?' I look around, trying to see why he's gone so rigid, but nothing is out of place.

'Recruiters are here. We have to hide.'

'What?' I can't have recruiters finding me now. 'Where?'

'Take my hand. *Quickly.*'

Two men dressed in black suits walk around the corner towards us just as Hunter's hand latches onto mine. They stand tall and straight, their hair slicked back and their faces cold and impassive. Their eyes stare right through me, like I'm not here at all.

One icy set of eyes connects with mine, without any evidence of recognition or perception that I am here. They quickly continue on as they scope the parameter of the yard. It doesn't look like they can see us.

In unison, the two men walk their stiff, abrupt steps towards us. I can feel sweat on Hunter's palm as he firmly grasps my hand.

As they near, my breathing stops all together. One of them passes, but the other slows his march. His nostrils flare and his eyes flicker in our direction. I close my eyes and grasp Hunter's hand tighter. I can hear the man's slow breaths, in and out, in and out. The whole world goes silent, except for these constant measured inhalations.

The man's boot scuffs as he moves on. I peek one eye open, and then the other when I see it's clear. A door slams shut behind us and I turn to look at Hunter again.

His face is still taught with concentration, but his eyes are no longer distant. He looks at me and leans his lips down to my ear. 'We should go.'

I don't know whether it's Hunter's lips being so close to my ear, or the nervousness I felt because of those men, but the words send a shiver down my spine. I haven't ever seen Hunter act like this. He seems afraid. I know he doesn't want to go to the north, but I didn't realise he was this desperate to avoid it. Unless of course he knows they will send me to the west when they find me? He pulls at my hand to get me moving.

As we walk away I take a look inside the window of the classroom the men have just entered. The two of them stand at the front of the room watching the class. I spot Lara and my stomach drops. Her head is down as she concentrates on writing, but I can see her hand quivering from here.

'C'mon,' Hunter whispers, urgently tugging me. I look at him, confused. His eyes flick towards the classroom. 'There's nothing you can do,' he says when he spots Lara. 'If you tried anything you'd only make it worse.'

I look back at her one last time, before allowing Hunter to tug me away. I thought being recruited to the north was a good thing? Surely it's not bad enough to warrant his response?

As we move further away from the classroom a cheer erupts from inside and my stomach plummets. Has Lara just won the genetic lottery and been recruited to the north?

CHAPTER FIFTEEN

Hunter refuses to let me go to my last class for the day. I try to tell him I'm at no risk of being recruited, but he gives me a dark glare and tells me, in no uncertain terms, I am not allowed to head back to class, which only makes me more concerned he knows the truth about me.

We spend the last hour of the day sitting under a large tree, down by the netball courts, watching a group of younger students as they play. Hunter is distant and withdrawn. He hasn't said anything since we saw those men walk into Lara's classroom.

As our silence lengthens my mind is overcome with worrying thoughts about Lara. I keep seeing her sitting at her desk, her hands shaking as she tries to avoid detection. She'd lied about her talent and kept it a secret from me for so long, not even Sophie knew how talented Lara is. I should've realised she didn't want to be recruited, what I can't understand is why.

'Hunter?'

'Yeah?' He doesn't turn to look at me in response.

'Hunter,' I say louder, causing him to snap to attention and turn to look at me.

'Why don't you want to be recruited?'

'I've told you this be—'

'I know. But I've never seen you so nervous before. What's the real reason?' I ask, cutting him off before he gives me the same excuse as last time. He watches me guardedly before taking a deep breath and explaining.

'I guess originally I didn't want to be recruited for the reasons I explained to you before. I didn't want to let yet another decision be taken away from me. That, of course, was before I became curious.' He pauses as if searching for the right words. 'They make being talented sound so amazing. I mean, you've seen the kids around school and how much they worship the talents. It's like the best thing that could possibly happen.'

He chuckles darkly under his breath. As if it's the world's biggest joke. 'So, I kept an eye out. Well, more I kept my mind open and read people I encountered. I was trying to see if I could pick up on what exactly happens over there. I didn't have much success, but then one day I read one of the recruiters. He must've been fairly high up because I saw a series of images; tests they were running.'

'You think they experiment on the talented?' I ask.

'Maybe. But I think it's worse than that. I think they were testing modifications of talented abilities on untalents and talentless. I think they want everyone to be talented. It's like anything less isn't good enough.'

'What?' I exclaim.

'I don't know for sure. The images I'd seen were pretty quick, and I didn't really get a clear idea of what was happening. All I know is there's a reason why they keep the talented on the north side of the river, the untalents in the east and talentless in the west. I can assure you it's not just because some people are more special than others. I don't want to be a part of whatever they've got going on.'

I stare at him, not knowing what to say. What he saw must've been pretty disturbing if he's this worried about it. If it's true, I can't blame him for wanting to stay as far away from the recruiters as possible.

'Could the tests they're doing make people ill?' I ask. 'Is it what they're doing to the talentless at that hospital in the west?'

'How do you know about the talentless being sick?'

'I've been over the wall and seen the people who live there.' What I fail to mention is the fact I will be joining them any time now. The thought makes me want to throw up. My time here is running out.

'Yes, I think that's why,' he responds.

'I need to check on Lara,' I say, as the bell signalling the end of the day rings.

'Wait, before you go, there's been something I've been meaning to ask you...' Hunter says, as he stands up. He reaches his hands down to help pull me up too.

I pat off the grass that clings to my jeans. 'Ask me what?'

'I was wondering if you want to bump cuffs with me?'

'Oh,' I look down at my CommuCuff. 'Sure.'

He takes a step closer to me, his body nearly touching mine. I crane my neck back to look up at him.

'I just thought, you know, seeing as how we're friends and all. I should probably get your username.'

'Right,' I breathe. I feel the gentle 'clink' as he bumps his cuff against mine.

'Now that wasn't so bad @ElleWinters, was it?' he asks, looking down at my details.

'No.' I swiftly look down as @HunterBlake registers on my cuff. When I look up I find Hunter staring at me.

I take a step back from him and look over towards the locker room. 'I should go...'

He looks as though he wants to argue with me, but after everything he's just told me about being recruited I'm worried. I need to know she's okay. 'I'll see you tomorrow,' I say, leaving no room for debate.

When I get to the lockers, the rush of students that usually crowd the room at the end of the day is over. I stand by Lara's locker waiting. As the minutes drag by the school becomes quieter and I begin to get the feeling she's left for the day.

As I head out the front gates of the school I attempt to comm her. She doesn't answer though and a flicker of worry and doubt rushes through me. I feel rattled. Our last conversation hadn't been exactly friendly and then with the recruiters in her lesson... What if something's happened?

A set of pedestrian lights flick green up ahead and I jog to make sure I don't miss them. I'm surprised at myself as I get to the other side of the road. A few weeks ago I either would've been amazed by the lights, or not realised what they were and proceeded to play chicken with any cars on the road. Now they are so ordinary. I guess I'm really beginning to adapt to life up here.

As I slow back down to a walk, I catch sight of Lara's high pony-tail bobbing along further down the street. 'Lara?' I call out to her, but she doesn't turn. 'Lara!' I yell out louder, running to catch up with her.

'You're okay,' I say, grinning as I fall into stride with her.

'Yes,' she replies, not looking over to me. My stomach muscles clench as I look at her. She's pissed off.

I grab a hold of her arm and stop her. 'Can I please talk to you?' I ask.

She shrugs her shoulders and looks away from me. I ignore her indifference and drag her over to the alcove of one of the apartment buildings.

'Are you okay?' I ask.

She folds her arms and leans against the wall. 'I'm fine.' She turns her head away from me again, out towards the street.

'I saw the recruiters in your classroom, they didn't notice you or anything?'

'No,' she says. I watch her for a moment trying to gauge what's wrong.

'But someone got recruited?'

'Sophie did,' she responds, still refusing to look at me.

'Oh.' Sophie will be pleased. I hope she'll be safe over there, especially considering everything I've just heard from Hunter. I guess she'll be better off in the north than I'll be in the west when they finally find me.

Lara looks as though she's about to walk off so I quickly interject. 'I'm sorry. I didn't mean the things I said earlier today,' I say, guessing she's upset because of the way I acted at lunch. 'I've just been so overwhelmed by everything that's been happening. I didn't ever want to upset you. You just don't know what it's like being up here with all these people who can do these things you can't do. It's hard.'

'You want me to feel sorry for you because you're untalented?' she asks, looking at me incredulously. 'You keep saying how hard it is for you, not being talented, not being able to do things—I get it, it can be scary. But as hard as you think you've got it, you've got nothing on how scary it has been developing this talent.

'Can you imagine breaking down crying in class, because you're feeling someone else's sadness? Or starting a fight because you're feeling someone else's anger? Or worse, when I would feel something. Like last weekend when we went to the loft and I got so angry I caused an all out brawl. You think you have it bad, but you really need a reality check.'

I stand in stunned silence.

'Lara, I had no idea—'

'Of course you wouldn't,' she says, cutting me off. 'These "talents" aren't everything you think they would be. They're scary and daunting, and I'm only just beginning to get a grip over mine. You have *no* idea what it's been like.'

Her eyes are welling with tears. I can't believe how selfish I've been. I'd never even thought about what it would be like to be talented. I raise my hand out to her arm, but she knocks it away.

'I don't want your sympathy. It's suffocating...' She turns and walks away down the street. I want to follow her and tell her the truth about why I've been behaving the way I have, but it's clear she wants some space and I can't stand the idea that my emotions only make it worse for her. I need to get some control over my feelings before I try to fix things.

I sink down to sit on the step and watch as people walk past. I feel as though the truth about my escape from the ARC is slowly catching up with me. With the recruiters checking for talents at school, it won't be long before they inspect one of my classes and I'm found. I don't want to be taken to West Hope, especially after seeing the people that live there, but I can't spend the rest of my life skipping classes and hiding from recruiters. My time in the east is running out and I have to do something quickly if I want to find Sebastian.

I sit on the step thinking about what to do next until after the sun has set and darkness has descended. I shudder as the cool night air seeps into my bones. The wind whisks around the city streets and licks my body with its icy waves of cold air.

I huddle my arms around my body and try not to think about my warm jacket, still hanging in my locker at school, exactly where I'd left it. The cold and the ache building in my head indicate it's definitely time to go home. I gather myself and begin slowly walking back.

I'm almost back to the Mason's apartment building when I see Hunter walking towards me. His eyes light up when he notices me.

'Hey stranger,' he says, as he approaches. 'Where have you been?'

'What do you mean?'

'I've just been at the Mason's place to check you got home safely after the recruiters today. They said you weren't back yet. I was beginning to worry...'

'I'm fine I just stopped for a while on my way back, taking some time to think,' I say.

'You look freezing,' he notices, looking down at me rubbing my own arms. He takes his jacket off and places it over my shoulders. The warmth of his body still coats the inside of it and I instantly feel respite from the cold. I look at him guiltily though and try to shrug it off.

'I can't...' I say, trying to give it back, 'and I'm nearly home now.'

'Don't be silly. I'm fine. Seriously, I've got a sweater in my bag if I get cold.' He firmly places the jacket back over my shoulders.

'Thanks. I forgot mine at school. Are you sure you don't mind?' I check one last time.

'Not at all.' He begins humming as he walks with an irritatingly smug grin plastered across his face.

'You're in a better mood than this afternoon,' I say.

'I don't know what you're talking about.'

'You're grinning ... and humming. You don't hum.'

'I do when I'm around you,' he replies.

'Oh! I think I just threw up in my mouth a little bit.' I put my hand over my mouth and pretend to gag, which earns me a glare.

'So, did you really just want to check up on me, or have I gained myself a stalker?' I ask.

'You are very stalkable,' he jokes. 'But, unfortunately, I'm not here stalking today. Actually, I've been thinking about your friend Sebastian.'

'You have?' I stop in my tracks and face him.

'Yeah. I think we may be able to find out where he is,' he says, turning to face me.

'How?' I can barely contain my excitement.

He looks up and down the street before he continues. 'I was thinking about Lara's idea to contact M to get Sebastian's location.'

I frown at the information he obviously gleaned while I was at his place and try not to get upset. 'Go on.'

'Nobody knows when the next loft party will be after the way the last one ended. It's probably a much better idea we go to the reintegration centre to get the information we need. They hold files on everyone who's in the ARC and on the surface. Technically there should be a file on Sebastian which shows where he's gone.'

'How do we...' my voice trails off and I look him in the eyes. 'You want us to break in, don't you?'

'Breaking in is such a harsh way of putting it—'

'We're not doing it.' I cut him off before he gets any further ideas. 'No way, are we doing it. It's way too dangerous.'

'Elle, we do have a slight advantage,' he says, tapping his forehead.

'Nope. Not going to happen,' I say, firmly. 'It was scary enough with those recruiters today. Besides, I'm fairly certain I know where he is.'

'You are? Then why are you still looking for him?' He looks at me exasperated.

'Well, I don't know for sure, but I'm pretty certain. And I would've gone to check myself, but I don't know how to get there.'

'Where do you think he is then?'

'The north side of the river,' I respond.

He gives me a calculating look. I can almost see the cogs whirling around in his mind as he considers what I've said.

'You can't go there,' he says.

'Why do people keep saying that? What's the big deal with over there?'

'For starters, untalents aren't allowed on that side of the river. Even if you get there it's dangerous. From what I understand, the energy of having all those talents in the same place makes the air unstable, and it's difficult for untalents to handle.'

'Would you be okay if you went there?'

'Yeah I've been there before.'

'Why can't you just go for me then?'

He looks at me uncomfortably, guilt touching his eyes. 'Because it's risky for me...'

'Risky how?'

'Risky because my talent might be sensed, and there won't just be one or two recruiters' minds to be manipulated, but many. You know how I feel about the north...'

'No, you're right. I don't want you taking that risk.' I chew down on my lip. 'Listen, I'm more than happy to go myself, I just don't know how to get there. I tried to walk to the bridge, but it didn't work out so well. If you could just tell me—'

'What do you mean it didn't work out so well?'

'I tried to walk to the bridge so I could get to the north, but it was strange. No matter how long I walked, I never seemed to get any closer to it.'

He shakes his head as he listens. 'I've never heard of that before. It sounds like something new they've implemented... Anyway, it doesn't matter, you're not going by yourself.

'Listen,' he says, taking hold of my shoulders. 'I will come with you if we find out Sebastian is definitely over there, but I'm not letting you go alone. And we will only risk it if we can be certain he's there.'

'You think breaking into the reintegration centre is the answer?' I ask.

'Elle, we'll be in and out of there so quickly. It will be fine.' He lets go of my shoulders and we start slowly walking down the street again.

'What happens if we get caught?' I ask.

'We won't,' he replies.

'Seriously, Hunter. I want to know the risks. What would they do to us?'

He looks at my face and considers me before he continues. 'They'll probably just give us a slap across the wrists.'

I've been watching him closely, and he isn't telling me everything. It's obvious there's more to this than he's letting on. 'Okay, worst case scenario, what could happen?' I ask.

'Worst case? They send criminals to the farms.' He lowers his voice as a man walks past us.

'What farms? That doesn't sound so bad.' I always loved spending time in the plantation.

'Trust me, it is. The living conditions are so poor and the labour so hard people actually die out there. And those that survive the conditions ... well, you can imagine what some of these criminals do for fun.'

I gulp, wishing I hadn't asked. I definitely won't look at my food the same way again.

'This doesn't seem like a very good idea,' I say. *Horrible idea* is probably a more appropriate description. If I'm sent to the farms I'll never find Sebastian. Not to mention that, with a complete lack of talent, I'd be totally unable to protect myself. He's not doing a very good job at convincing me.

'That was, of course, *worst case*. I highly doubt they'd send minors out there. Don't you want to know for certain where Sebastian is? I mean, how sure are you he's in North Hope?'

West Hope still hasn't been ruled out as an option and there's never been anything that shows he's in the north conclusively. I guess I'm not certain he's there. 'You're right. I'm not certain,' I reply. 'You really think we won't be caught?'

'Elle, I wouldn't take you if I thought we would. Besides, I know a guy who can help.' He glances down at his cuff as he says this.

He knows a guy, yeah, that definitely reassures me. I'm really not happy with his plan, but Hunter would have a better idea than I do about how dangerous his idea is. 'When do you want to do it?'

'Tonight.'

'You don't think that's rushing into it a little fast?' I ask, as he checks his cuff again. The way he keeps looking at it I get the impression this plan isn't quite as spontaneous as he's making it out to be.

'No, I don't. Why? Do you want to wait and do this another time?'

I shake my head. There were recruiters at school today and they might be back tomorrow. I may not have that much longer to try this. 'No, let's not wait,' I say. 'You're right, we should do it tonight.'

He grins in response. 'Okay, let's do it.'

'And you think this will work?' I ask.

'Yeah I do, but first you need to tell the Masons you'll be at Lara's tonight and then we've got a few stops to make.'

CHAPTER SIXTEEN

'Hunter, this is a bad idea...' My eyes flicker uneasily to the doorhandle in front of us. It's not nearly as bad as his idea to break into the reintegration centre, but it's up there.

Hunter leans against the doorframe, a wicked smirk playing at the corners of his lips. It's the kind of irritating look that deserves a good slap across the face.

'Stop stressing, she'll forgive you. She'll be able to tell how sorry you are, so she has to. You are sorry, aren't you?' he jokes.

'Yes. Of course I am.' I clench my hands into fists to try and quell the anxious energy pulsing through them. There's nothing funny about this situation. I've really upset Lara, and she wants space from me right now. We shouldn't be here.

Hunter impatiently knocks on the door again. As we continue to wait his knocking gradually becomes an insistent banging. I'm about to suggest we leave when Lara finally answers. She doesn't look happy to see me. In fact, she looks like she's about to shut the door in my face.

'Lara, I'm really sorry.' The words rush out of my mouth before she slams it shut.

'Lara...' Hunter warns. 'Give her another chance. You know she's sorry.' Lara looks at me guiltily and nods.

'I'm sorry too,' she says. 'I know you never had any real problem with who I am. I've just been upset all afternoon about the recruiters and I took it out on you.' I step forward and hug her. I hate that having a talent has been so upsetting for her.

When I step back she's smiling.

'Aw, now we've all made up let's get down to business,' Hunter says.

'What are you guys doing here?' Lara asks.

'We're breaking into the reintegration centre to find out where Elle's friend Sebastian is. You keen?' Hunter replies, in a hushed, steady voice.

Lara looks over her shoulder cautiously. Then stares back at Hunter for a moment. 'You think that's a good idea?' she says, her eyes still focused on Hunter's. I look back and forth at the two of them as something unsaid passes between them.

After a moment Lara's eyes slip back into focus and she looks back at me. 'What are we waiting for?' she asks, grabbing her coat off the hook on the wall. She calls out a quick goodbye to her sister as she slams the door shut behind her.

'Did I miss something?' I ask, as we head back down to the street.

'I just told her what I told you telepathically. It's quicker that way, and Lara doesn't mind,' Hunter explains. He won't look at me in the eye as he says it though, so I'm not certain I believe him. I've got a feeling that Lara and Hunter have ulterior motives here, and they are united in keeping me in the dark about it.

Once we're outside Hunter leads us away from the bright lights and bustling noises of the busy intersection. Instead, we make our way into a quieter, darker area of the city. Without the bright and busy hubbub I've become accustomed to, the streets take on an eerie abandoned quality.

The street lamps are dimmer in this part of town and the few cars parked along the edge of the road are old, rusty looking things. I'd be surprised if they even worked anymore.

Hunter stops in front of a wide, brick apartment building. It's only a few stories tall, with small slits for windows and a rickety looking fire escape that zig-zags across the face of it.

'Stop number two?' I ask Hunter, quietly. The words had been only just louder than a whisper, but it's so quiet here that I feel like the sound could travel for miles.

'Yeah. We need to deal with these.' He lifts his wrist up and points to his CommuCuff. 'The guy who lives here is talented. He can manipulate electronics.' I give him a confused look. 'You'll see,' he adds.

We push through a glass door at the front of the building and enter a small entrance foyer. Our reflections stare back at us from a mirror that covers the wall at the end of the room. I look away from myself, unable to reconcile with the fear I can see in my eyes.

'This way,' Hunter calls, waving us over to the stairwell door he props open.

Several flights of stairs later we arrive at a long carpeted hallway. The building has a modest interior, but it is by no means as dilapidated as Hunter's building. It feels homely compared with the generic, clean lines of the Mason's.

Hunter walks confidently to one of the doors and knocks loudly.

'Gadge ... It's me,' he calls. The door opens a crack and jars as the chain lock that stretches between the door and the frame reaches its limit. The two large eyes of a short, squat man peer through it. He looks like he's in his late twenties, maybe his thirties.

'Hunter?' he asks, his eyes darting nervously between the three of us.

'Hey man. What's up?'

'Not much,' he stutters. He closes the door and detaches the lock, before swinging the door open wide.

'Wh—what do you want this time Hunter?' the man asks, as

Hunter pushes past him and into the apartment. Lara and I shoot each other a questioning glance, before following him inside.

The apartment is small and messy. The open kitchen and living area we walk into is an absolute pigsty—actually, even pigpens in the ARC weren't this messy. There is a mountain of dirty pots, pans and plates covering the food-stained, once white kitchen bench. Several bags of garbage sit on the floor next to a bin that is overflowing with filth. I try to breathe through my mouth to avoid the rank smell, but it doesn't help much.

The living area isn't as bad as the kitchen, but it's still not great. The curtains hang ragged from the window frame, and the couches are weighed down by piles of clothes that have been strewn all over them. The coffee table is completely obscured by plates, bowls and cups. It's like this man has never put anything away before in his life.

'I was wondering if you could disable the GPS on our Commu-Cuffs?' Hunter asks, once Gadge has shut the door behind us.

Gadge looks at Hunter thoughtfully. 'I could...' he ventures. 'But they'll know something's up if your signature disappears completely.'

'They track us with these?' I ask. Lara and Gadge turn and look at me like I've just stated the most obvious of obvious.

Hunter laughs and then explains, 'The Government don't actively watch everyone, but they can bring up a log of where you've been.' He turns back to Gadge. 'Can you suggest anything then?'

Gadge paces up and down, drumming his fingers against his lips.

'How long do you need them disabled for?' he asks.

'Tonight should be fine,' Hunter replies. Gadge walks to the corner of the room and unearths a tablet, which is buried beneath a pile of loose wires and circuit boards.

'I can hack the system and override your GPS, so it won't locate you. I'll divert it to register your position to your most visited location, which will probably be your home. It will just look like you haven't left the house.'

'And that would work?'

'I don't see why it wouldn't.' Gadge approaches me first and takes my hand, lifting it so he can look closely at my cuff. He twists it around my wrist before he places his hand across the face of it and closes his eyes.

His top lip twitches and a slight frown creases his forehead. I glance over at Lara who looks about as confused as I feel. He doesn't look like he's doing anything other than trying to give himself a headache, let alone hacking into a computer system.

We wait in silence for minutes before he gasps loudly, his eyes flicker back open and a smug grin forms on his lips.

'All done,' he says. 'Next.' He does the same for others' cuffs and when he finishes with Hunter's he says, 'I've diverted them for 48 hours. That ought to give you enough time, but it's not so long they'll become suspicious about the inactivity.'

Hunter gives him a grateful pat across the back. 'Thanks, man. I owe you one.'

'Yeah, I'll just add another one to your IOU list,' Gadge mutters to himself as he walks us to the door.

Once we're back outside we continue walking briskly. We turn down several more streets and I lose any idea of where we are. The area is deadly quiet and as we walk the buildings become increasingly derelict and deserted. Most front doors are boarded over and many ground floor windows have been smashed in. It's even worse than the area where the loft party had been the other night, more like a part of West Hope than East.

'Do you really think Sebastian's file will say where he is in Hope?' I ask, trying to distract myself from the uneasy feeling I get as we walk through a dim area, where the street lighting has gone out.

'Yeah,' Hunter replies. 'They keep track of everything. It's just a matter of finding it that's the problem.'

'Have you guys been back to the reintegration centre since you arrived?'

'No,' Lara replies.

'I have,' Hunter says. Before I can ask him about it he picks up the pace and walks out in front of us. Lara glances at me nervously as we follow him. What isn't he telling us?

We walk for nearly an hour to reach the reintegration centre, as Hunter takes us there via the outskirts of the city. I pull Hunter's jacket in closer, and wrap my arms around my body, as the building looms up ahead of us.

It looks larger than I remember and, as I take in the size of it, I begin to worry. Even if we get in I have no idea how we'll be able to find anything. Lara and Hunter are relaxed as we walk closer, but I can feel my heart pounding in my ears. Surely this is more dangerous than crossing the river.

We all stop once we're across the street from it and head a few feet down a side alley. It's out of sight but still provides a reasonable vantage of the building. There are fewer lights down this end of town, and I'm grateful it's slightly darker.

Hunter turns to us both. 'There's an entrance down the side of the building and I think that will be our best way of getting in. You both stay here, I'm going to have a look around.'

'Are you sure we should be splitting up?' I ask.

'Winters, are you worried about me?' Hunter jokes.

'No,' I respond, quickly. He wiggles his eyebrows at me and disappears across the road.

The seconds drag by as we wait for him. After ten minutes I begin to get really worried.

'You're making me nervous,' Lara chides.

'Oh, sorry. I can't really help it you know.' I take a deep breath in to try and still my nerves. I hadn't realised my emotions would be affecting her.

'Just like you can't help how you feel all warm and fuzzy when Hunter's around?' she asks.

'I don't know what you're talking about,' I say, unable to look her in the eyes. Instead I focus on the other side of the road, waiting for a sign from Hunter. I'm happy when I'm around him but by no means all 'warm and fuzzy.'

She suddenly laughs. 'You should see your face.'

I spare a moment to glare at her before returning to watch for Hunter. 'You're not very funny. We're supposed to be keeping an eye out for Hunter.'

'At the very least I was able to distract you from being nervous. It's much nicer when you're not.'

Hunter appears next to the building and waves us over. I relax at the sight of him, which is obviously just because I'm glad he hasn't been caught—nothing else.

'It's time to stop teasing me for your amusement now,' I say, nodding my head in Hunter's direction. Her face quickly becomes more serious.

'Okay. Let's go.'

CHAPTER SEVENTEEN

Hunter leads us down a long dark alley, which runs the perimeter of the reintegration centre. Up ahead, a spotlight shines down on a large, black shadow of a man. I suspect this is a guard as he paces the short distance between a doorway and the tall, corrugated iron fence bordering the alleyway. I can't shake the feeling in my gut that this is a bad idea.

As we approach the guard his head jerks up and he looks directly at me. I shiver as his dark eyes pass over mine. A long, thick scar runs down the length of his cheek and he looks at us with a deadpan stare, which I imagine would make most people uncomfortable.

The man's eyes glaze over as Hunter begins to manipulate him. This does nothing to ease my concerns. If anything, it makes him look slightly crazed. The guard turns to punch a code into the door. As he does, I catch Hunter's eyes. They seem to sparkle with excitement, and I can feel a similar sense of anticipation building inside of me as well. The keypad lets off a short 'beep' as the code is accepted. The heavy door clanks as the locks are released.

We enter the building through a corridor containing rich,

mahogany walls that feature large portraits of people in the strangest clothes. I almost feel as though they are watching me as I pass. I attempt to dismiss the thought, instead focusing on the lone doorway we walk towards at the end of the hallway.

Hunter approaches the door slowly and, taking the handle in his palm, he cautiously turns it, treating it so carefully you would've sworn it were made of fragile glass. As he pulls the door back it makes a sudden loud creaking noise. Hunter automatically stops pulling and we all hold our breath.

Surely someone heard that.

I close my eyes and listen carefully for movement. All I can hear is the steady, nearly inaudible breathing of Lara and Hunter. After minutes of standing in silence, Hunter continues to pull the door open with one swift movement.

We peer out from behind the door to see a large open space before us. The ceilings are lofted and a second floor balcony runs the perimeter of the room. The idea of entering such an exposed area makes me nervous.

'I read the guard's mind, so I know there are filing rooms up on the third floor, which contain the hard copies of all the data we're looking for,' Hunter whispers. He looks at the shiny, silver lift prominently placed down the other end of the room.

'I think we'd be safer taking the stairs though.' Hunter points across to the other side of the room, where a brightly lit, green sign indicates the stairwell.

Taking long, careful steps forward Hunter checks the coast is clear. He stops a few meters in to look around the room, his hand held out to us in a clear 'wait there' fashion. After a moment he frantically waves us over, and with silent steps, we slip across the foyer and into the stairwell.

I ease the door shut behind me and take a deep breath to try and calm my rapidly beating heart. We haven't even seen another guard since the one at the entrance, but it doesn't mean they're not here.

We climb the stairs to the third floor and make our way into a long hallway, lined with doors. There must be dozens of rooms leading from here, and the sight leaves me feeling rather helpless. We could be here all night if we don't know which one we're looking for.

Hunter barely pauses as he proceeds to enter the hallway. He looks at the number on the door closest to us before moving on, so he must know the room we need. Lara shrugs at me, as if to say, she's just as lost as I am.

We leave the safety of the stairwell to trail after Hunter. Moments later, there's the unmistakable sound of the elevator door opening and several sets of boots stepping onto the hardwood floor.

I face the noise and see four men, in identical guard uniforms, stepping out from the open elevator.

'Hey!' one of them yells.

I turn back to Hunter and Lara. We have to run if we don't want to be caught, but seconds pass and Hunter doesn't move as he stares the men down.

'Hunter!' There's a pleading edge to my voice, begging him to do something, anything, other than just stand there. The sound wakes him and when his eyes come back into focus, he grabs my hand, then Lara's arm, pulling the two of us back towards the wall.

'Stay as still as possible,' he whispers, before closing his eyes. His whole face transforms with a look of total concentration. Lara also looks like she's concentrating. She stares intently at the men who bear down upon us, and her eyes flicker with sparks of brilliant purple, as she uses her talent on them.

I try to stay as still as possible, but I can feel my heart racing faster as I listen to the men's feet, pounding against the floor as they run towards us. Lara and Hunter's bodies are completely rigid as they use their minds to protect us. Are they really capable of dealing with all four guards?

I squeeze Hunter's hand tighter. *Please be able to do this.* I want to help so—I freeze. My whole body becomes a statue as two guards walk past, barely inches from where I stand. I stop breathing and the hairs on my arms stand on end as one of their arms brushes past mine. Slowly I move to push my back harder against the wall.

The guards don't look at us though. They stumble along looking confused and disorientated, almost zombie like as they amble away from us, having completely forgotten we're here. That's if they even know where 'here' is!

Once they pass, I turn to look for the other two men. One of them is lying completely still on the floor, while the other one glares at us with pure loathing. His eyes are like ice and I shudder at the sight of him. He takes slow, determined strides towards us. Each step is heavy and laboured, almost as though he's wading through a pool of water.

His eyes begin to wander off every few steps, and he shakes his head violently before turning and looking back at us. He's trying to shake off whatever spell Lara and Hunter are trying to put him under and he's succeeding.

'You'll have to try harder than that,' he says, through gritted teeth. 'I can still see you.'

Sweat drips from Hunter and Lara's foreheads, but their efforts are not enough. The guard has slowed down, but he's nowhere near to stopping. I turn away from the man to search for something that can help and spot a fire extinguisher hanging from the wall further down.

Without giving myself time to consider what I'm doing, I shake my hand free from Hunter's and make a dash for it.

'Elle!' Hunter yells, as I run away from him. I don't look back. I don't have time. I wrench the extinguisher from the wall and turn back to the guard, who is still resolutely staggering towards Lara and Hunter. He's closer to them now. Much closer.

Lara starts gasping, as though she's running out of breath. She grabs her hands to her throat and her eyes look to the guard with a desperate plea, begging him to stop.

The guard stands taller and walks forward with greater ease, a smug leer tugging at the corner of his lips.

I run back towards them, fear for Lara giving me strength. Silent tears run down Lara's cheeks as her body collapses down against the wall. Whatever he's doing, he's suffocating her!

'No!' I scream lifting the fire extinguisher over my head. The man looks up at me in shock, but before I can bring the fire extinguisher down, his body flops onto the floor where he lies completely still.

I stare at the lifeless body. Is he dead? A wave of nausea rolls through me and I drop the fire extinguisher on the floor.

Bile rises in my throat and I tear my eyes away, unable to look at the body that lies so still on the floor in front of me. What were we thinking coming in here?

Lara coughs, which draws my attention away from the man. She's slouched against the wall with her legs curled up and cradled in her arms. She looks even smaller than usual.

'Are you okay?' I ask, as I rush to crouch beside her.

'Yeah,' she replies, her voice sounding hoarse. 'He was just so strong. I couldn't stop him.'

I look over my shoulder to his unmoving body. 'What did you do to him,' I ask Hunter.

'He's just knocked out,' Hunter says. 'I can still sense his mind,' he reassures, but there's a strange look in his eyes. Is he lying? I shake my head and look at him grimly. What was I thinking? This was a bad idea.

'What about the others?' I ask.

'He's sleeping,' Lara points to the other man on the floor.

'And the other two think it's happy hour and time to knock off,' Hunter replies.

'But they're okay?' I check.

'Yeah, they'll be fine.'

'We should keep going,' Hunter says. I don't move. I can't stop looking at the man on the floor. Even though I didn't end up hitting him with the extinguisher, it feels like it's my fault the guard is laying there so still. Lara takes a hold of my hand and gives it a reassuring squeeze.

'He'll be fine,' she says. I help her stand up and we begin to slowly make our way down the corridor. I feel sick the entire way.

Eventually, Hunter slows to a stop. He looks around and then walks over to one of the doors. He punches a code into the keypad and pulls down on the handle. The door opens and he calmly steps into the room.

As we enter, Lara switches on the light, and a sea of filing cabinets greet our eyes. I quietly shut the door behind us.

'How did you know...' My voice trails off as I realise how stupid that question sounds.

I walk over to the cabinets and quickly find my way to 'S'. I wrench back the drawer to find a series of folders crammed into it.

'Scott, Scott, Scott.' I mumble as I flick through the names. 'Found it!' I whisper excitedly, as I pull a folder from the drawer.

Well, almost. It's April's file. I glance over at Hunter and Lara who are both looking through cabinets too. Maybe that's why they were so eager to break in here?

I open the manila folder labelled April Scott. The first page is a picture of April, the April I'd known, all wide eyes and mousey hair. My heart aches as I look at her. Being taken has changed her so much.

I sadly flick past the first page to look at the rest of the file. There are only a few pages to it, but my eyes are drawn to the bold words written across the top of the second page—'Talented Level 7.' Surely this is wrong?

I riffle through the other pages for some sort of explanation, but it doesn't give me much to go on. She has been so secretive and acts so differently; maybe this is why?

I continue reading the file. It lists her current location as unknown. Originally, she had been placed in the talented dormitories, but she had run away just months later. I shake my head, confused. This doesn't make any sense.

I quickly place the folder back into the cabinet. I don't have time to try and figure April out. We need to get out of here as soon as possible and I'm wasting precious time.

The folder behind April's is Isabel Scott's. I desperately want to check it for what has happened to her, she'd been like a mother to me growing up, but I don't have time and Sebastian's folder in directly behind it. Relief washes over me as I pull the file from the drawer. I can feel a goofy grin beaming from my face. It's the first confirmation I've had that he's definitely up here.

Taking a deep breath, I open the folder to find Sebastian's face smiling back at me from the front page. I touch the picture lightly with my fingers. He's really here.

'Elle, hurry up.' Hunter presses me. I look over and both Hunter and Lara are standing near the door. Hunter's arms are crossed and his feet are tapping impatiently.

'Sorry,' I whisper back. I skip past the first page and move straight on to the second. There in bold are the words I'd almost expected to see, 'Talented, Level 9'. I want to read on, and find out more about what he can do, but Hunter clears his throat. I scan the page quickly for where he lives, and almost jump with excitement when I find the address. Block 4, room 2D, talented dormitories. I repeat it in my head several times, making certain I commit it to memory.

I slip the file back in the cabinet and shove the drawer shut.

'Finally!' Lara exclaims, as I come to stand next to her.

'He's in the talented dormitories. It says he's a level nine—' My voice goes silent. The muffled beeping of a code being entered into the door reaches my ears, followed by the distinctive click of the locks being released. The door swings inwards to reveal a guard standing there.

'What are you kids doing in here?'

Hunter and Lara look to each other, terrified. Barely a second passes and their eyes are both closed, their brows firmly furrowing.

'Hey! Where'd you go?' The man looks around the room, fervently. He takes several cautious steps into the room, his arms out wide, his fingers grasping at the air. He lifts his face up into the air, his nose wriggling as he inhales.

'I know you're still in here,' he warns. Hunter grabs a hold of me, bringing me closer. Silently we shuffle backwards until our bodies are up against the wall.

'You're not the only ones who are talented. I can smell you in here...' He stops sniffing and looks directly at me.

My breath catches in my throat and I hold as still as possible, not daring to make a sound. Still, he stares. I know he can't see me, but I swear he's looking *right* into my eyes. I continue to hold my breath and pray he looks away.

His eyes slowly move on towards Lara.

'Come out, come out, wherever you are,' he sniggers, as though he's enjoying the hunt. I take an involuntary step forward, as he nears Lara. She looks like she can barely stand.

He inches closer to Lara and reaches his hand out towards her. His fingertips just scrape past her hair and his lips curve in a demented sneer.

'Got ya!' His hands claw towards her face and just as he grabs a handful of hair his body slackens and his outstretched arm falls limply at his side. He abruptly stands up straight and turns away from us, looking thoroughly confused.

'I could've sworn I'd seen people in here...' He looks around the room curiously, before shrugging his shoulders and walking out, closing the door behind him.

Hunter's body slouches and I grab him so he doesn't collapse. When he looks at me, I see beads of sweat on his forehead and his nose has begun to bleed.

'Are you okay?' I ask.

'I'm fine.'

'But your nose—'

'I'm fine. Go check on Lara,' he says, putting a hand out to lean against the wall.

Lara is slouched over, her hands resting on her knees. 'You don't have to worry so much,' she says, without looking up at me. 'We'll both be fine if you give us a moment to recover.'

'We may not have a moment,' I respond. 'We need to leave now, before they come back.'

Lara nods her head wearily and stands tall. As I move back to help Hunter, I hear a commotion out in the hallway. There's the sound of yelling and footsteps slapping against the hard wooden floor. All of our heads turn to look at the door.

'Elle, come here,' Hunter says, firmly holding his arm out. I go to him and slide my arm under and around his body, helping support his weight.

Once we're steady, I look up and am surprised to see Lara still standing near the door. She looks exhausted, but her face is full of determination.

'They know we're here...' Hunter says, his voice strained.

'We don't have the strength. Let me do this,' she says. Hunter nods in response.

'What are you talking about?' My voice quivers with fear. 'Lara...'

She doesn't respond, instead she turns towards the door.

'Lara, what are you doing?' I ask. Hunter pulls me into him and wraps his other arm around me.

'You have to let her go,' he whispers in my ear. *What?* I try to shake Hunter off me, but his arms hold me firmly.

'Lara, no!' My voice is muffled by Hunter's shirt.

'Elle, please, you have to be still,' Hunter implores. I continue to try and shake him off, but it's useless. Even in his exhausted state, he's still so much stronger than me. I turn my head towards the door. Lara still stands there, just watching the doorway. What is she doing?

'Lara...'

I hear the beeping noise of a code being entered into the door's keypad, and my body stops wriggling and freezes still. Someone else is coming in.

The door slowly opens and a man's shocked eyes come to rest on Lara standing in front of him.

'There you are...' He roughly grabs Lara by the arm and shakes her.

'Thought you could break in and get away with it?' he says. She looks at him calmly and allows him to shake her. He yanks her out of the room. *No.* I try to yell and scream, but the sound doesn't come out of my mouth.

The man's eyes scan around the room, running straight by us, before shutting the door behind him as he takes Lara away.

I listen to their footsteps slowly disappearing into the distance. Silent angry tears run down my face.

Hunter slowly releases me, his body slumping against the wall.

'How could you?' I say with disgust. 'How could you let her take the fall for us?'

He looks sad and guilty. 'She found something on her dad...' he says. 'She's been trying to get in contact with him for so long. She didn't have time to explain, but she asked me to give her a chance to go...'

'She wanted you to make sure I wouldn't stop her?' He nods, lowering his eyes to the ground. I can't believe what's just happened, but there's no time to argue about it now.

'She didn't want to put you in any more danger,' he says.

'Me in danger? I'm the selfish one who put you both in danger.'

'Elle, it was my idea. Lara and I both had our own reasons for coming here and Lara is capable of looking after herself. If anything, I put you in danger.'

'That doesn't matter now. We have to go help her. Where did she go?'

'No, we're not going after her. She doesn't want that. C'mon, we have to go. I'm completely drained, and we need to get out of here before I can't protect you anymore.'

'Hunter, we can't leave her behind,' I plead.

'She wanted this, and she'll be fine. She did it so we could escape. Please don't let what she's done go to waste,' he begs. I look at him. He's right, he can barely stand, he's completely exhausted and he looks like he could collapse. Even if we find Lara, Hunter is in no state to be able to do anything.

'Okay,' I concede, the word tasting foul in my mouth. This whole situation feels wrong. I can't believe we are abandoning her, leaving her in the hands of that guard.

I move to the door and put my ear against the wood, listening for movement in the hallway. It's completely silent out there, so I open the door a crack. Then, when I still don't hear anyone, I open it wide and take a hesitant step out of the room. The coast is clear.

I help Hunter up and, ever so quietly, we hurry back to the stairwell we'd used to get up here earlier. We try to move quickly down the stairs, but Hunter is struggling to walk. Each laboured step gets heavier and our pace continually slows. We're almost at the ground floor when the voice of a man echoes above. We both look up at the sound. The man's feet scuff along the concrete steps of the stairway just above us.

'Run!' Hunter whispers.

Half running, half dragging Hunter, we burst out onto the ground floor. The guard has heard us and is shouting from behind. Hunter is stumbling badly as he attempts to run. His movements are sluggish and he leans on me heavily.

'C'mon,' I cry, tugging him to move faster. The security guard is behind us now, shouting into his cuff. My legs burn as I try to move quicker, struggling as I help support Hunter.

We sprint towards one of the doors and barrel through it to the hallway filled with portraits. As we tear around the corner we finally find the door to the exit before us.

'Hunter, we're almost there.' I feel giddy with anticipation. We can do this! We can make it.

A guard steps out in front of the doorway, and my stomach plummets as all my hopes are dashed. We're completely boxed in.

I start to slow down and stop, to try and figure a way around the man, but then he completely surprises me by turning towards the door to push it open for us. In the doorway stands the guard from earlier, who stares at the man like he's grown a third eye. We rush past him. Hunter looks even weaker, if that's possible. His face is dazed and his eyes are distant as he continues to try and control the guard.

'Let him go Hunter, you need your strength,' I beg, when we're halfway down the alleyway and far enough away that we should be able to escape.

I hear one guard yelling at the other for letting us get away, and feel slight relief Hunter's not using any more energy. I worry he's gone too far though, his face is drained of colour and he looks positively white.

We race across the empty street and into one of the side alleys. I can't hear anyone behind us and, glancing over my shoulder, I see there's no one pursuing us down the alleyway. In the silent night our quick, rough breathing and our pounding footsteps against the pavement are all that fill the air. There's a flood of adrenaline passing through me right now, but I know it won't sustain me for long.

For ages we twist and turn down a maze of streets and alleys. When my legs start seizing up, and my body comes close to collapse, I know I can run no further. I take a look behind us. There's no one in the long stretch of alley we've just run down and I feel pretty certain we've been able to get away.

As I turn back around, I notice Hunter's knees shuddering. His feet are tripping over themselves and he's practically crumbling as he attempts to keep up. I'm amazed he's made it this far.

'Stop,' I wheeze, taking hold of Hunter's arm and pulling him to a stand still. We both crouch over, resting our hands against our knees, as we attempt to regain our breath.

'We should keep walking,' Hunter says, between his gasps for air. He appears disorientated and doesn't look like he's in any state to continue, but he's right. We're too obvious standing out here in this deserted part of town.

I sling his arm over my shoulder and try to support him as we walk. Now we've slowed, I take more notice of my surroundings. Not that it's much help. I'm completely disorientated and can't find my bearings. I can't even use my GPS to find my way home.

Hunter weighs heavily down on me and already I struggle to keep him upright. There's no way, in this state, we'll be able to make it across the city tonight.

When we reach the end of the alley, I spot a park across the other side of the road and guide us towards it. It's nothing like the one near the Mason's. The trees and bushes are overgrown and wild. There are no manicured rose gardens or maintained grass lawns here. It's perfect for what we need though—just a few hours resting and we should be able to make it back home.

I begin looking for a sheltered spot, where we won't be found, and eventually come across a patch of grass surrounded by bushes. We should be able to recover here, safely hidden from anyone who may be searching for us.

I ease Hunter down onto the ground and sit next to him.

'Thanks Elle,' he mumbles, barely able to form the words.

'That's okay.' I've barely responded when he collapses back on the grass, asleep. With him lying there, safely recovering, I notice for the first time I'm shaking. My head pounds like crazy and I feel nauseous.

I stand up and walk to the other side of the bushes to keep an eye out, desperately hoping the waves of sickness stop now we've found somewhere to hide for the night. Unfortunately my body has other ideas and, without warning, I throw up.

If I felt terrible before, I feel a whole lot worse now. Exhaustion sweeps over me as I make my way back to Hunter. All the adrenaline that had been coursing through me just moments ago has fled.

I collapse on the ground next to him. I want to stay awake, to keep watch in case we've been followed. However, my head keeps nodding forward, waking me up as I fall in and out of fleeting moments of sleep. I can't remember ever feeling quite so tired...

MY NECK TWITCHES and my eyes fly open. I'm lying down, curled in a ball on the ground. *Damn it!* I can't believe I fell asleep.

I look up to see the stars twinkling against the night sky and I feel a rush of relief. It's still night and I didn't sleep until morning.

I try to sit up, but I become acutely aware of something heavy across my waist. I peer down to find Hunter's arm slung over it. His deep, heavy breaths steadily come from behind me, so I can tell he's still sleeping.

I take hold of his arm, lifting it up, so I can roll out from underneath it. I place it back on the ground and sit up.

He looks so innocent when he sleeps. None of his usual cocky, arrogance is evident on his face. It feels weird to watch him sleeping, but I feel so drawn in by how peaceful he looks. I could never stare at him this way when he's awake.

'Was it as good for you as it was for me?' he murmurs. I gasp and grab my hand to my chest.

'I thought you were sleeping!' He laughs drowsily and opens his eyes. With one long yawn he then stretches out on the grass.

'Now how could I sleep when I'm lying next to someone who snores as loudly as you?'

I raise one eyebrow at him and punch his arm playfully. I turn away and look around at the bushes that surround us. It's so cold and damp out here, and now that I'm not huddled next to Hunter my body starts to shiver. I hug my arms around my legs and pull them into my chest.

A twig snaps nearby and my head whips around to look in the direction the sound came from. My heart beats faster and my breath is caught in my throat. Have they found us?

'It's just a bird,' Hunter says, sitting up next to me. 'No need to freak out.'

My body slouches with relief, but my mind is still alert. 'We've been here too long. It's not safe...'

'We're okay. There's no one close by,' Hunter says. 'Besides, I'm sure they've given up the search by now.'

I look around uncertainly. I want to be reassured by his words and to feel safe we won't be found; but it doesn't matter how safe we are when Lara's not here with us. We should've stuck together.

'Lara didn't tell me she was still looking for a way to contact her dad,' I say.

'We all have our secrets,' Hunter responds.

'Yes, we do. What were you searching for in those cabinets?'

Hunter hesitates before he responds. 'I was trying to find out about my mum, but I should've realised there wouldn't be a file on her.'

'Why not?'

Hunter shrugs. 'I just should've,' he mumbles, looking away from me like he doesn't want to talk about it. I don't want to push him to talk about her if he doesn't want to.

'We shouldn't have gone there tonight,' I say, almost as much to myself as to him.

'You got the information you were after...'

'But at what cost?'

'Lara will be fine. I'm sure at worst she'll get hours doing community service.'

I shake my head. What we did was *really* bad and those guards were brutal. I don't feel so certain she'll just get a slap across the wrist.

'Elle?' I look up at Hunter. 'She'll be fine,' he says, with complete certainty.

I give a small nod. He'd have a better idea than I do and he seems so sure. 'I just hope you're right. I don't know what I'll do if she's in real trouble.'

Hunter leans over and takes one of my hands in his. 'I promise, no matter what, we will make sure she's okay and nothing bad happens to her.'

I look into his eyes and I believe him. The way he's looking at me, it's clear how much he cares. As I stare at him, something changes in the way he looks at me, causing my heart to beat a little faster. I no longer feel like he's thinking about Lara anymore.

I quickly drop my eyes from his. 'We should probably get going.'

Hunter takes a moment before he stands and holds out his hands to help me up. 'Come on Winters,' he says, slinging his arm over my shoulders. 'Let's get you home.'

CHAPTER EIGHTEEN

L ara's usual seat next to me in maths sits disturbingly empty. She should've been at school by now. Honestly, she should have been here hours ago.

I rub my tired eyes and place my head down in my hands. Other than the short nap I had while I was hiding out with Hunter last night, I haven't had a wink of sleep. Hunter and I only managed to get back to his apartment this morning and it was a rush to try and get to school for the day.

The bell rings and I quickly gather my things. I make a fool of myself when I stumble over my feet in my rush to get out of the class-room. I should stop worrying. Lara will be fine.

'Hey, Winters,' Hunter says, as I walk out the door. He's leaning against the doorframe, his messy hair dangling down over his eyes. Despite his casual stance, he looks worried and I'm only more convinced of this when he pulls me aside, allowing the other students to file out past us.

'What's wrong?' I ask, my mind already jumping to bad, worst-case-scenario conclusions.

He looks around at the other students and begins to pace away from them. 'Lara didn't turn up for class this morning,' he says, when we're safely out of earshot.

'Yeah, she was meant to be in maths with me just now.' I take a slow breath to calm myself, which doesn't work. 'What if they didn't let her go?'

'We shouldn't jump to any conclusions.' He takes a seat at one of the tables on the grass next to the cafeteria building. 'She may have gotten home late and decided to sleep in...' he says. I doubt he's convinced himself with that line and he's definitely failed to even slightly convince me.

I sit across from him, dropping my bag down on the table. 'We both know they took her last night. What if they've done something terrible to her?' I ask, hushing my voice as other students walk past.

'I read the guard's mind. He was more concerned with his own skin than the law and didn't want his boss to know some teenager got past him. I highly doubt he would've taken it further than a good talking to. I honestly think she's just at home,' he replies, with more certainty this time.

'You were so exhausted though, how can you be sure?'

'Elle,' he says firmly.

'And she hasn't been answering my comms...'

'Elle!' he says louder. 'Lara's avoided detection for a long time. She can look after herself. I'm sure she's fine.'

'Okay,' I mumble. He doesn't *know* she's fine. Maybe I should ditch my last class to go check on her?

Hunter's eyes cloud over and I can tell his mind is no longer focused on sitting here with me. I look down at my hands and clasp them together to stop them from fidgeting.

Something feels off. Maybe it's just because I'm worried about Lara, or maybe it's nothing? I just can't shake the feeling there's something wrong.

Hunter's eyes focus back on me, and I open my mouth to welcome him back, but he stands stiffly and roughly grabs a hold of my arm. He tugs me to follow him and I have to jog to keep up.

'Hunt...' I begin to ask what's wrong, but the reason for his sudden movement comes into view across the quad. One of the men in suits is back. A recruiter.

Hunter steers us to the front gates of the school and out, all the while retaining the firm grip he has on my arm. I can practically feel how scared he is as we head away from the school.

He continues walking and doesn't stop until we reach the park near the Mason's apartment. Once we've entered the park, he slows to a stop by the large, grassy field and then turns to me.

'I'm sorry I freaked out back there,' he says, his voice unusually subdued.

'Hunter it's okay, I know how you feel about them—'

'Feel about them...' he repeats, with a dry, humourless laugh. 'Elle, he was there for you.'

I gasp and grab my hand to my mouth. He marches away from me angrily, running his shaking hands through his hair. His obvious frustration is palpable.

'Why? How?' I stutter.

'They know you're a level one. He was there to relocate you to the west.'

'Oh.' I take a step back from him and cross my arms over my chest. I'd been waiting for this day to come and it finally has. 'Mr. Kale warned me this might happen. I've been expecting it, but didn't think it would be so soon.'

'You knew they were coming for you?'

'Don't sound so surprised... I only wish I had more time to find Sebastian.'

'You're not going back there. I'm not letting them take you to the west.'

I shake my head. 'I don't have a choice. They'll be able to track me with this again tomorrow,' I say, lifting my cuff up to show him. 'There's nowhere to hide.'

Hunter takes a slow, deep breath in and then out. 'Let's go across the bridge.'

'What?' I almost yell. He walks over and takes my hand.

'We may never get another chance. Our GPS functions are disabled and who knows what will happen tomorrow.'

I shake my head profusely. 'Hunter, that's crazy. You've barely recovered after last night and I don't want you risking yourself for me.' I touch his arm lightly. 'Finding Sebastian is my responsibility and you've already helped me more than I could've hoped for. Just because the recruiters are planning on taking me to the west, doesn't mean we should do anything stupid...'

'No, it's not stupid. You said Sebastian is a level nine talent. If we find him he may be able to help you with the recruiters.'

'We don't know what he can do though.'

'I've only ever heard of two other nines ... just trust me, he'll be able to help.'

'But—'

'Elle, stop trying to argue with me, I've made my mind up and we're going.' He begins stalking away towards the riverside. I jog a few steps to catch up and silently walk beside him.

When we reach the pathway that runs alongside the river, the bridge comes into view ahead. Again it looks so close. So close that surely it wouldn't take more than a few minutes to reach it. Hunter doesn't miss a beat as he continues striding towards the bridge.

'I tried this the other day. It doesn't get any closer,' I say, as I try to keep up with Hunter's charge.

'*I* didn't try the other day,' he says.

I glimpse up at him from the corner of my eye, nervous to look at him directly. The way he walks is fierce and his face is determined. There's almost an angry recklessness to him right now. I try to ignore it, but it worries me. We shouldn't be doing this now.

I look ahead to the bridge. It's still the same distance away and we're not getting any closer. It's just as I expected. 'Hunter, this isn't working...'

He stops and walks over to the trees that line the pathway. I follow quietly behind him.

'You don't see it?' he asks, turning to me as we reach the coverage of the trees.

'See what?'

'We're just by the entrance to the bridge now,' he says, looking out over the water.

'No, it's just as far away as before,' I protest.

He considers my face and scrunches his eyebrows thoughtfully. 'You mustn't be able to see it because you're an untalent.' He smiles at me apologetically as he leans up against a tree and folds his arms, contemplating what we should do.

'I know you don't want me playing around up there,' he wiggles his fingers in the direction of my forehead. 'But if you let me, I should be able to allow you to see what I see, and hopefully there won't be any issue with you crossing.'

'I don't know,' I reply.

'You could just follow me, but you won't be able to see the bridge, and if you can't see the bridge, you'll be walking through thin air. There are guards standing on either end, and if you can't see them, they will know something's up,' he points out.

'It doesn't sound like I have much choice,' I mutter, looking down at my feet as I scuff them across the dirt. This all still seems like a bad idea.

'Elle, you always have a choice,' he says, leaning towards me. 'I won't do anything you don't want me to do.' I look up at him, meeting his gaze, and there's such sincerity evident in his eyes that I know I can trust him with this.

'What do I need to do?'

'Nothing really. It might be easier though if you hold my hand.' I raise my eyebrows, questioning him, which makes him laugh.

'It makes it easier for me to affect what you're seeing, and I need to conserve as much energy as possible,' he explains, holding out his hand.

I start to reach out to him, but then quickly pull back. 'You don't think that maybe we should wait until it's dark?' I ask.

'No, it will raise less suspicion if we head across in the daytime.' He looks down at his watch. 'Besides, we need to be back across the bridge by nine because of the curfew in the north.'

'Okay.' I place my hand in his and look up into his eyes, waiting to feel differently, to notice his influence over my mind, but there's nothing.

'It's not working, are you sure you're doing it right?' I worry. He laughs and points to the distance. I follow the direction of his hand and gasp.

'The bridge!' I exclaim. I fight the urge to rub my eyes. There, just fifty meters away, is the bridge. From this close I can make out the ornate design that runs across the railing and the tall stone figures that stand proudly in the middle of it.

Two guards pace either side of the pillars that mark the entrance. Behind them is the stone walkway that curves up and over to the far side of the river. It was there all along.

'This isn't too much effort?' I ask.

'Nope.' Hunter gives my hand a squeeze and we begin walking towards the bridge.

One of the guards notices us as we approach. His whole demeanour stiffens and a frown crosses his forehead. As I look past him, I begin to understand why he's bracing himself. The bridge is deserted of people.

I want to ask Hunter why no one is on it, but we're too close to the guard now to say anything. I feel jittery as my nerves kick in.

'We haven't been notified of a crossing,' the man says, when we get to him.

'I'm not surprised,' Hunter responds. 'We only just got the order ourselves. They're expecting us at the academy.'

He scratches at his head, confused. 'I'll need to verify it with command...'

Hunter glances at his cuff. 'We're already running late. Can you scan our cuffs and verify while we cross? If there are any problems you can always comm the guards on the other side.'

'I suppose that should be fine. If you could raise your cuffs...' the man orders, indicating for us to place our cuffs against the scanner he holds. I try to remain composed as Hunter calmly raises his cuff towards the man. The scanner doesn't touch the cuff, but the guard nods as though it has and turns to me. Before the scanner touches my cuff the guard nods again at the scanner.

'Everything appears to be in order,' he says, standing back and indicating with his hand for us to continue. 'There shouldn't be any problem with you crossing Sir.'

We pass the man and move onto the bridge at a steady pace.

'Sir?' I ask, under my breath. 'What did he mean?'

'I manipulated him into thinking I was someone else. That way, he won't contact command.'

'And it worked?'

'Apparently.'

As we near the other side my head begins to feel heavy, like each thought is slow and laborious to think. I feel sleepy and my eyelids sag in response.

Hunter is absolutely fine. When he looks at me though, a flash of concern touches his eyes.

We reach the end of the bridge and pass another set of guards who salute Hunter. Finally I've made it to North Hope. It's quiet here, and the cobbled stoned streets and ancient stone buildings make this place feel darker than the east. There are no flashy skyscrapers and the narrow roads are empty of cars. The few people roaming the sidewalks keep their heads down as they hurry about their business. It appears to be almost deserted.

'This way.' Hunter tugs my hand and sets off down one of the roads.

'Do you know where you're going?'

'Yeah. I've been to the talented dormitories before,' he replies.

'You have?'

'Yes.' His tone of voice firmly puts an end to any further questions I may have. He lets go of my hand. 'I shouldn't need to mess around with your head anymore,' he mumbles.

'It wasn't so bad.' Aside from seeing the bridge, I couldn't even tell he'd been doing it. I take a quick glance behind me as we go around the corner. Amazingly, the bridge has vanished, just like magic, and once again the river flows steadily in its place.

As we walk deeper into the empty area of the city my legs feel heavier and each step I take is harder. I'm exhausted after last night and my body appears to be running on less than empty. We are crazy to be doing this right now. I wish we could've waited until we'd both recovered.

I keep walking, trying to ignore how tired I am, but my feet begin to stumble unsteadily beneath me.

'Do you think we could rest for a moment?' I ask, exhaustion getting the better of me.

'It's not much further,' Hunter replies. He stops though when he looks at me. He must be able to tell how worn out I am.

'Shit,' he mutters. He quickly grabs a hold of my hand and my fatigue lessens. Soon I barely feel tired at all.

'What are you doing?' I ask. I feel amazing, compared to a few minutes ago.

'Do you remember what I said about what it's like for untalents over here?'

'Yes.'

'That's what was happening to you. The energy the talented give off is very powerful. When so many are gathered in one place it can have this effect on untalents. Maybe we shouldn't stay here too long,' he says.

With Hunter holding my hand we continue on, with a renewed sense of urgency. I can't let him drain his energy to protect me. What if we run into trouble? We need to find Sebastian fast and get out of here.

As we turn around a corner Hunter abruptly tugs on my arm and pulls me down an alleyway. We walk deep into the dark shadows of the alley and then he pulls me down low to crouch behind some wooden pallets.

'What are we—' Hunter places one finger against my mouth to silence me.

'Recruiters,' he whispers, effectively causing me to freeze. 'They'll be suspicious of anyone like us outside the dorms.' The minutes drag by and I barely even breathe. When it seems safe, I crane my neck to look over the pallets and check what's happening. There's a man beyond the alley on the other side of the road. He looks like he's... Hunter grabs my shoulders and pulls me down.

'What are you thinking?' he whispers urgently. 'He'll see you!'

I shake my head. I still feel the urge to stand up and try to get closer to the man. Is he doing this to me?

I return to being a frozen statue, but the recruiter must've seen me because moments later there's the echo of footsteps entering the alley. My heart beats faster and faster as he draws closer. I look over at Hunter for reassurance, but his eyes are wide with panic.

He drops my hand and I immediately feel exhaustion overwhelm me. I lean back against the alley wall and watch him, praying he'll know what to do. His eyes focus and the smallest flicker of a violet flame dances across them.

The recruiter continues to move closer. Through a gap in the pallet, I see his feet come into view just on the other side of it. I can hear his slow and steady breaths. He's heading straight towards us and clearly knows we're here.

He appears from behind the pallet and stands so close to where we hide he only has to look down to see us. I draw back against the wall and hold my breath, waiting for him to turn and find us. He doesn't though. He doesn't even look like he's searching for us anymore. His body has become rigid and his face has a blank expression across it. After a few moments, his shoulders relax. He breathes a long, calm breath out, lights a cigarette and turns to walk back to the main road.

He stays by the entrance to the alley for a while before moving away. Even after the man has disappeared from sight, Hunter stays crouched in his position, his eyes completely vacant of any expression.

Finally his eyes slip back into focus. 'He's gone, but we've lost a lot of time,' he says.

I stand and stretch my legs out, trying to release some of the stiffness in them after spending all that time stuck in the same position. Hunter looks drained and I feel guilty as I take hold of his hand again. I want to tell him to turn around and go back to the east without me, to let me finish this alone, but I know how damn stubborn he is. Hunter would be more likely to chop off his left arm than give up now, and he doesn't even know Sebastian.

When we emerge from the alleyway, dusk has settled over the street and the lamps that line the road flicker on. I clasp Hunter's hand tighter, worrying at how much time has already passed.

The road becomes steep and when we reach the peak of the rise we come across a tall iron fence that borders a wall of thick, unkempt bushes. Using a footpath just beside the fence, we follow it until we reach a set of large metal gates.

'We're here,' Hunter announces.

Through the thick wrought iron bars stands a large mansion, set back from the road. A dirt and gravel driveway lined by overgrown hedges winds its way up to the building, where two men in suits are illuminated by the porch light that shines out over the front yard. They stand in a relaxed fashion by the entrance to the house. More recruiters, I assume. I glance up at Hunter, nervously, but he doesn't seem too troubled.

'If we keep to the shadows of the trees lining the drive I should be able to handle two,' he reassures me. 'What block was he in?'

'Four,' I respond, automatically. I rack my brain trying to visualise the file. 'Yes, definitely four,' I confirm.

He nods and goes to push open the metal gate.

'Stop!' I whisper, grabbing his arm. Another recruiter appears from around the side of the house to join the other two.

'It's pretty dark, it won't take much mind control to handle another one,' he replies.

'Shhh!' I pull him back from the open gate. The new recruiter's stance is oddly familiar. I wait with baited breath for him to turn so I can see his face more clearly.

'Elle, I said it's fine—'

'Shhh!' I hush him again, my eyes glued to the new recruiter. Where do I know this person from? If he would just show his face...

The recruiter turns to point at one of the cars by the front gate and my breath catches in my throat.

I know that face. I'd know that face anywhere.

Ryan.

'What is *he* doing here?' I whisper.

'You know that recruiter?' Hunter asks, darkly.

I nod in response. 'He was in the ARC with me. Although it's pretty obvious now I didn't *know* him well at all.'

I watch him closely as he talks to the other two recruiters. It all makes sense now. He was always disappearing and knew things the rest of us didn't. He'd hidden the fact he was an official from me, so should I really be surprised?

He begins to walk away from the other two and I follow his movements. Once he's several feet away from them he stops in his tracks, and stands still for a moment, before vanishing.

'What?' I say, a bit too loudly. I rub my eyes and look back at the empty spot I'd just seen him in. 'Did I really just see that?'

Hunter laughs and goes back to pushing open the metal gate. 'And you say you've watched Talented,' he jibes. The laughter doesn't reach his eyes though and he looks more uncomfortable than he did before. Maybe even he is intimidated by Ryan's talent?

'But where did he go?' I ask. Hunter shrugs in response.

He pulls me into the compound and instead of being nervous or scared I feel consumed by shock at what I've just seen. Ryan must be extremely talented. Can it really have been him? And if it was, what is he doing here?

Hunter sticks to the shadows under the trees as he leads me down the driveway. I grasp his hand tightly and hope like hell he knows what he's doing.

The guards don't look at us as we walk towards the house. As we get closer, Instead of heading for the front door, Hunter directs us around the side. 'The dormitory blocks are round back,' he whispers.

The side of the house is cloaked in darkness and I stumble often as we make our way down the pathway. Hunter, on the other hand, is remarkably steady as we blindly wind through a maze of bushes.

As we near the back of the house bright lights come into view up ahead. The whole area is lit up like it's daytime. There's a large open quad and behind it there are four buildings, which are several stories tall, standing in neat rows. The square is filled with young people joking about and relaxing at tables.

There are no numbers obviously displayed on the buildings. 'Which one is four?' Hunter silently points at the building that lies on the far right.

'And how do we get past all the people out there?'

'We blend in. Come on.' He ignores my look of concern and tugs me towards the crowd.

Walking through the yard I can feel eyes all over me. My skin tingles as the talented students watch us pass. *They know.* They have to know. Why else would they be watching us like this?

I glance up at Hunter to take my cue on how to act. He's relaxed and at ease as we walk past the many watching eyes. I take deep breaths and try to mimic his cool façade. It's not as easy as it sounds and I'm quite certain I look as frightened as I feel.

I grip his hand tighter as a guy struts towards us, looking like he owns the place. 'Hey man,' he says to Hunter. 'You new around here?'

'Yeah,' Hunter replies. 'Recently recruited.'

The guy appraises us both. 'I'm Nick. I'm like the welcoming committee,' he says, laughing at his personal joke.

'Great,' Hunter responds.

'What's your talent level?'

'Eight,' Hunter says, instantly.

'And your talent...'

'Mind manipulation.'

The guy looks impressed. 'And the girl?' He nods his head in my direction.

I grip Hunter's hand even tighter.

'She's a six,' he says.

'What's her talent?' Nick looks at me directly for the first time. He tilts his head as he watches me, his eyes searching mine. 'She doesn't feel like a six.'

I lift my chin up and meet his stare. 'Well I am,' I say, hating being talked about like I'm not here.

'If you say so.' He scratches his head and looks away, appearing to have lost interest in me. 'I guess I'll see you both around.' He turns and walks back to a group of people sitting at one of the benches. My shoulders sag with relief as I watch him leave. That had been close.

Hunter tugs my arm sharply, walking quickly as he leads me away. I glance back at the boy as he sits back down at the bench filled with kids. I'm almost certain he could sense I'm not talented. I shudder and look away. *Way* too close.

We walk around the side of building number four. The bright lights of the quad don't reach this far and it's a relief to be hidden in the dark shadow of the building. I run my hand through my hair and peer around to check we're alone. 'How did they know?'

Hunter looks over his shoulder before turning back to me. 'No one recognised our faces. There are a lot of people out there with a lot of different talents. Many were able to pick up on the fact that no one knew us. It magnified the fact we were strangers.' He shakes his head. 'I didn't expect that to happen.'

He slumps forward suddenly.

'Hunter, are you okay?' Panic races through me as I try to prop him up.

'Sorry, I'm fine, really.' With great effort he tries to stand himself

185

upright but falters, collapsing back onto me. I help him over to the wall so he can sit down and lean against the building.

'I had a lot of people probing us out there and it took a lot of energy to make sure they didn't know we were from the east and you were an untalent. Convincing that guy to lose interest in you was especially hard work. He knew there was something different about you.'

I look at his body sagging down and the amount of effort he's expending just trying to sit up against the wall. This was a bad idea. We shouldn't be here. I've put Hunter in too much danger doing this.

'I'll be fine in a minute,' he says.

'No. You need to stay here and rest while I go inside.' We're right by the entrance to the building now. It shouldn't be too hard to get to Sebastian from here.

'I'm not staying here. You need me,' he says, trying to stand back up.

I place my hand firmly on his shoulder, stopping him from standing, and then lower myself so my face is level with his. 'No, I need you to try and recover. I'll be fine. I just need to find room 2D. Easy.'

'If I'm out here I won't be able to mask the effects the talented are having on you. It'll be especially bad here where there are so many.'

'Stop it now. I can handle it. I don't want you draining any more energy.' He shakes his head, refusing.

'Hunter...' I command.

'Okay,' he says, quietly giving up. He's so exhausted he barely has the energy to fight me on this, and I think deep down he knows it's the right thing to do. 'Just remember, the energy of all the talents only affects your mind. Your body won't actually be as worn down as it feels...'

'Hunter, it's fine.'

I'm about to repeat myself to him, to make him stop helping me, when I stagger forward. I feel like a brick wall has fallen on top of my shoulders. My body aches and all I want to do is curl up next to

Hunter so I can go to sleep. It takes all my willpower to ignore it and stand strong.

'Let's get you over to those bushes before I go inside. I don't like the idea of leaving you lying here out in the open,' I say, my voice sounding steady, despite how weak I feel.

It takes several minutes to help Hunter to the safety of the bushes. Every step I take feels like I've run a mile. When he's finally propped up against a tree and tucked out of sight I face the building.

'The sooner you're out of there the better,' Hunter stresses to me. 'If anything happens to me, I want you to leave immediately. Don't let the recruiters find you.'

'Nothing will happen, and I'll be as quick as I can,' I respond, my heart fluttering with excitement. The fear and exhaustion are still there, but my body's adjusting to the feeling and now I also feel the thrill of hope. Sebastian is in the building standing right in front of me—I just know it. It feels like only yesterday that he was taken away from me in the ARC, yet I've learnt and grown so much in our time apart, and today I will finally see him again.

I take one look back to where Hunter is concealed behind the bushes and feel a twinge of guilt at leaving him. I've come this far though and he is safely hidden. I can't go back now. I turn resolutely and push open the large wooden doors to building four.

CHAPTER NINETEEN

M y heart thuds loudly in my ears as I climb the narrow, never-ending stairs to the second level of the building. Each step feels heavier than the last and I struggle to keep myself from feeling distracted by the fuzzy hum that vibrates through my mind.

I remind myself it's only in my mind and continue up the stairs with the knowledge that each step brings me closer to Sebastian.

I lean heavily against the doorframe when I reach the second floor and take several deep breaths. I'm surprised at the effort each small movement takes. Hunter had been right in warning me about the effects of other talents. And he doesn't even know just how untalented I am.

When I open the door to exit the stairwell I'm confronted with a blast of music coming from the far end of the passage. People spill out of one of the rooms and are milling throughout the corridor.

I chew down on my bottom lip as I take in the scene. Hunter isn't here to protect me from anyone who may suspect I'm untalented, but there's no way I can just turn around now.

One of the girls in the hallway half-turns and looks at me curiously. I'm standing in the doorway staring down the hall like some weirdo, so of course I'm going to draw attention. I take a few quick steps in and the door slams firmly shut behind me. Decision made.

On the door closest to me is a gold, metal '2V' that dangles just under the peephole. 2D must be down the other end, on the other side of all the people.

I nervously edge around the first group of kids who are hanging out down this end of the corridor. They're all chatting and laughing so loudly they barely even notice me walking by. Not to mention that several of the group are using the occasion to show off their talents. One girl is doing some weird trick with strange, large bubbles in the air, and another guy looks as though he's juggling small explosions like fireworks.

Room 2S, 2R, 2Q, I count as I walk on. A roar of excited claps and cheers erupts from behind me. I quickly glance over my shoulder as 'Mr. Fireworks' takes a bow.

I rub my eyes tiredly and try to focus back on task. It's not exactly easy though. My mind feels like a ball of thick putty, and it's near impossible for my thoughts to coherently wade their way through the mess and get to the surface unscathed.

The music slowly gets louder and the walls almost shake to the beat of the base. As I draw closer to the source of the blaring music my stomach lurches. I'm getting close to Sebastian's room number now.

2J, 2I, 2H. My heart beats faster. 2G, 2F. I'm now so close now. 2E...

I stop before 2D and steady my nerves. This may not turn out as planned. I close my eyes briefly and, taking a deep breath, I step towards the doorway.

The door is open and my stomach sinks. What if he's not here? I knock on the open door and take uncertain steps into the room.

'Hello?' I call out. No one hears my entrance though as the room is empty.

I stand with my feet cemented to the spot, staring at the empty space. He's *meant* to be here. My body begins to quiver and my stomach drops as reality sets in. Is he really not here?

I walk further into the room. Two beds lie unmade and there are clothes tossed indifferently across the floor. Sebastian was always hopeless at keeping his room clean, but it doesn't necessarily mean it's him. I try to find something familiar in the room, but everything is foreign and there's no way to be certain he lives here.

I will have to ask one of the kids out in the hallway. I don't want to draw attention to myself, but I don't have any other choice. I hear the deep sound of someone clearing their throat from over by the doorway. My head snaps around.

'Sebastian?' I whisper, barely able to speak his name, barely able to move.

'Elle?' he says. He looks at me like I'm a ghost. Like he scarcely even recognises me. He doesn't look happy, or sad. He just looks stunned.

I watch him nervously and with uncertainty, not knowing how to react. He seems so unsure about me being here.

'Hey Sebastian,' I say.

A massive grin spreads across his face and he bounds over, gathering me up in his arms. He squeezes me tightly, like he'll never let me go.

'It's so good to see you,' he says. I relax in his arms as all my doubt and all my worry fades away. I can't believe he's here, that I'm actually holding him in my arms.

When he finally pulls back I can feel wetness on my cheeks. I laugh, embarrassed, and wipe the tears away.

I stand back to look at him. He's matured so much in such a short time. His face is different and he almost reminds me of someone. Maybe he just looks more like his dad?

'Have you grown?' I say the first thing that comes to mind. He laughs and I smile along with him. I can't believe I've finally found him.

'Probably,' he says. He ruffles the hair on my head. 'But *you* obviously haven't.' I push his hand away, laughing.

'I can't believe you're here!' he continues, in disbelief. 'When did this happen? You were taken too?' he asks.

'Not exactly,' I admit, not wanting to delve into the whole saga right now. 'But how about you, I mean, how are you?'

'I'm great. Amazing. Can you believe we were stuck underground for all of our lives when we could've been living it up out here?' he says.

'Yeah some joke eh?' My response is cautious.

'The biggest. We were always so scared about being found tainted, and then being taken, when really it's like a dream come true.' He pauses for a moment while he stares at me. 'I just can't believe you're here,' he says again. He gathers me up in another hug and I laugh at his exuberance.

When he lets go of me this time we go and sit at the end of one of the beds.

'I'm so glad you've been placed in North Hope with me,' he says. 'You must be excited you're talented. What can you do? I can't imagine being untalented or *talentless* up here. How bad would that be?'

My blood runs cold as he says the words. They are said so flippantly he couldn't possibly know how bad it really is for people in the west.

'Yeah, the worst,' I respond, mechanically. He's looking at me with the boyish enthusiasm I've always loved, but it's different. He's different somehow.

'Have you looked for your mum or sister since getting up here?' I ask.

He shakes his head sadly. 'No, I haven't,' he replies, not quite looking me in the eyes. I reach my hand out to comfort him, but he quickly rushes on. 'I've been in talks to go on Talented. Can you believe it?' he says, changing the subject.

'Amazing,' I reply, pulling my hand back from him. Why hasn't finding his family been his first priority? 'What's your talent?' I ask.

'Sebastian?' A girl calls his name from out in the hallway.

He looks uneasily towards the doorway, then back at me.

'What...' I begin to ask a question, but lose my train of thought as a girl waltzes into the room. She is tall with short, spiky, white blonde hair, and long legs. I can feel my forehead crease with a frown as I look at her. She looks strangely familiar. I try to remember where I know her from and almost do a double take as I realise it's Chelsea, who was taken from the ARC just before Sebastian. He always said they were just friends, but the way she's looking at him...

'I was wondering where you—' She stops mid sentence as she notices me. Her face furrows, and a malicious glint flares in her eyes. If looks could kill, I'd be a goner after the glower she's just given me.

'What's she doing here?' she asks Sebastian. She looks me up and down before turning back to him. 'How about you just come find me when you're done?'

They're definitely not *just* friends. Sebastian and her are obviously something more. Her eyes flick over to me one last time, daring me to be offended. When I don't respond, she turns with a 'huff' and storms out of the room.

'Chelsea ... she's talented too?' I ask, turning to look at the far wall. I can't bring myself to look at him, as everything about our reunion seems to be going wrong. He's so clearly happy with his place in this new world and I would hate for him to see how disappointed I am.

'Yeah,' he responds.

I glance at him out of the corner of my eye and find he's watching me closely, as though he can tell how disheartened I am. It's disarming seeing him look at me that way and I quickly avert my eyes back to the far wall.

'Elle, will you please look at me? I'm so happy you're here. I thought I would never see you again...' he says. He goes to take a hold of my hand, but I quickly stand.

'I should go. It's a long way back to my side of the river,' I say, still unable to look at him.

'Your side?' I can hear the confusion in his voice, but I don't respond for fear of saying something I'll really regret. 'Elle?' he whispers. 'Are you talented?'

'No.'

He leaps up, taking hold of my shoulder, and turns me back to look at him. 'Elle, if you're untalented, you can't be here. We have to get you back across the bridge.'

'I'm such an idiot,' I murmur, decidedly ignoring him. 'I can't believe I came all this way to find you and bring you home, when it's obvious you're perfectly happy exactly where you are.'

'You want to take me back to your side of the river?' he asks, with total disbelief.

'No,' I respond. 'No, I'm not talking about taking you over the bridge. I'm talking about taking you *home*. You know, the one where your dad lives, where our friends live. Where we grew up. Remember that place?'

'What are you on about?' he asks, looking genuinely confused.

'I escaped from the ARC to come find you, to rescue you. All because I made some stupid promise that if you were ever taken I'd come for you.' Listening to myself say the words I feel so foolish. They sound like the actions of someone irrational and senseless, someone who doesn't think about the potential consequences of what they're doing.

'What did you do?' he asks me slowly, his tone thick with worry.

'You heard me.'

'Elle, please don't tell me you're not tainted.' His face goes white and he looks positively ill as he says it.

'I'm sorry the fact I'm talentless sickens you so much.'

'No. It's not that,' he says. He looks *really* worried.

'Then what is it?' I ask, the anger seeping from my voice, concern replacing it. My throat feels dry and I feel slightly nauseas. I have a bad, unpleasant feeling in the pit of my stomach.

'What is it?' I repeat.

'We have to get you out of here...' he mumbles to himself. 'Somewhere where you'll be safe, where we can get you the help you need.'

'Sebastian, you're scaring me.' He continues muttering to himself and I grab his arm, forcing him to look at me when he doesn't respond. 'What's wrong?'

'There's a reason why they keep people in the ARC. Why they don't bring everyone up to the surface...'

'Yeah, I know, something about the resources...' My voice trails off as I take in the apprehension on his face. 'That isn't the reason is it?'

'No, I wish it was. The truth is, people get really sick if they're not tainted and are brought to the surface,' he says.

'I'm fine,' I tell him.

His brow furrows and he slowly shakes his head at me. 'Maybe for now.'

'Sebastian, what are you talking about?'

He sighs sadly before he continues. 'People who come to the surface and aren't tainted they ... well they...' He scratches his head as he tries to think of the right way to explain. 'They become exposed too quickly and their genes mutate too rapidly.'

My heart feels like it stops beating and plummets down into the depths of my stomach. 'What do you mean?'

He looks away from me. 'I lied before because I didn't want to upset you. The first thing I did when I got up here was to try and find Mum and April. I can't even begin to tell you what I went through to get an answer. I couldn't find anything on April. It's almost like she came up here and disappeared. The last thing they had on file was her running away from the dormitories.'

He looks down and I open my mouth to tell him about her, but he continues before I have a chance. 'I was still trying to get information on my mum, which was so incredibly frustrating. I was getting nowhere, no matter who I asked. Then finally I found someone who could help me.' He looks at me, pain so transparent in his eyes.

'Elle, my mum was one of the first to be taken. Her blood result had been incorrect and she wasn't tainted.'

'What happened to her?' He looks away, unable to answer. 'Sebastian. What happened?'

When he turns to me his face is filled with such loss and despair. The way he looks at me, I know she didn't survive and there's no hope for me.

'She's dead,' he barely whispers. I step back from him and grasp my shaking hands to my mouth. 'But we'll find a way to stop it from happening to you. We'll find a cure and you will be fine. We just need to get you somewhere safe.'

'She can't be ... I can't be...' My voice trails off. How can Isabel be dead? I can't describe the emptiness I feel inside of me. I sink down to the floor and I curl my legs into my chest as angry tears fall down my cheeks. I give in to the torrent of emotions that rage beneath the surface, and allow them to overwhelm me.

I am vaguely aware when Sebastian sits next to me and pulls me into his strong arms, his voice making soft reassuring noises. Why didn't they tell us? Why did they have to be so secretive? If I'd known the truth I *never* would've escaped and come up here.

'Elle?' Sebastian says.

I slowly open my eyes. I feel drained and empty, like the person I am is no longer here. My bones ache in pain and my body feels limp and lifeless.

'I know you've got a lot to take in right now, but we need to get you out of here.' He turns my face to look at him and keeps a hold of it with his warm hands. Tenderly, he wipes away the tears that stain my cheeks. 'The time you spend in North Hope will only make you sick quicker. And we can't let the recruiters catch you. We need to get you back to East Hope, before they realise that you're here.'

'What do we do?' I ask.

His face looks just as lost as mine. 'First, we have to get you back over the bridge. Untalents aren't allowed over here and if they got there hands on you ... well, let's just hope they don't. When we get to

East Hope we'll come up with a plan. I know someone who might be able to help.'

I nod and allow Sebastian to help me to my feet.

A siren sounds overhead, the squeal it makes is so high pitched and loud I have to throw my hands over my ears. 'What's the alarm for?' I yell to Sebastian.

'We have to go, *now.*'

CHAPTER TWENTY

Sebastian grabs my hand and pulls me out into the hallway as the siren continues to blare throughout the building. He doesn't pause as we rush past the other kids, who all have their hands covering their ears to protect them from the piercing noise. One guy calls out to us, asking what the problem is, but Sebastian ignores him completely.

The cold night air hits me like an icy whip across the face as we push through the door that leads outside. I slip my hand out of Sebastian's and run over to the trees where I'd left Hunter earlier. He's nowhere to be seen though and there's absolutely no sign of where he's gone.

'Hunter's not here!'

'Who?'

I turn back to look at Sebastian. 'Hunter! He helped me get over the bridge to find you and wouldn't just leave without me. Where is he?'

Sebastian grabs my hand again and pulls me towards the quad. 'We can't waste any time looking for him. Elle, we have to go!'

'But it's my fault we're here.' I can feel my blood pumping quicker as panic sets in. 'He's talented and I can't let him get caught. We can't just leave him behind.'

Sebastian pauses for a moment and looks at me directly. 'If your friend is talented, he'll be okay. But *you* won't be if you're found, especially since you're not even tainted. Please Elle, trust me, we have to get you out of here.'

I swallow uncomfortably and nod my head. I can't believe I'm abandoning another friend, and I feel guilty as hell, but I don't know what will happen if the recruiters catch me. I have to make it to the east with Sebastian.

As we emerge from the dark shadows that line Sebastian's building, I feel increasingly unnerved. The quad is bathed in intense white light and completely empty. There's not a soul in sight.

'Where is everyone?' I wonder.

'In their dorms for mandatory check in.'

Sebastian looks over his shoulder before leading me out into the open space. It's incredibly difficult to remain calm when we're so exposed. I desperately want to get back to the cover of darkness.

We're halfway across when the siren signalling all over the compound stops, leaving the place in deafening silence. My ears ring and all I can hear are our uneven breaths and steady footsteps slapping against the concrete ground.

'Is it over?' I ask.

Sebastian shakes his head. 'Doubtful. If they know you're here, they won't stop until they find you. You're not allowed to be here and they don't take untalents coming to the north lightly.'

My grip tightens on Sebastian's hand and I desperately hope Hunter hasn't been found. If he hasn't been found it means he left me behind, but I struggle to believe he would do that, which only makes me worry more.

We slip into the darkness down the side of the main house and I'm more at ease once we're out of the bright lights. The danger is far from over though and every small sound I hear has me nearly jumping out of my skin.

'How will we get across the bridge?' I ask Sebastian. 'What will we do when we're on the other side?'

'I'll explain once we're closer,' he responds. 'We have to focus on getting out of the compound first, before they realise I'm gone. They would've shut the main gates by now and the recruiters will be checking the grounds.'

Instead of heading for the main drive, Sebastian veers off the pathway and into the bushes that grow wildly around the edge of the property. We climb and clamber our way through the overgrowth that often scratches my arms and legs, and snags on my clothes.

As I follow Sebastian I try to come to terms with everything I've learned tonight. I have to believe we can get to the other side of the river and there's a way to make me better.

I get a growing feeling Hunter has been found and he's the reason the alarm was raised. I know he's talented and capable of looking after himself, but I still worry about him and feel so guilty for leaving him behind. Sebastian didn't even give me a chance to try and find him.

When we reach the fence Sebastian holds his arm out, stopping me from getting any closer to it. 'The fence is electric, we can't touch it.'

I take a closer look at the network of wires. 'Is it to keep people in or out?' I wonder.

Sebastian doesn't hear me. He paces along the fence line, a look of focus and determination on his face.

'How do we get to the other side?' I ask.

He seems nervous as he stops pacing and turns to face me. 'Do you trust me?'

'Of course.'

He smiles and offers his hands out to me. I place mine in his, feeling the warmth of his skin as he closes his fingers around mine.

'Now, I need you to close your eyes and keep them shut until I tell you to open them.'

I frown, but do as he says. I want to peek, to see what he's doing and how he somehow believes he can get us to the other side of the fence, but I'm not stupid enough to do so when explicitly told not to. I wait in anticipation for something to happen, but nothing does, until I feel a slight rush of cold air. The moment happens so quickly though, I can't be certain anything has happened at all.

'You can open your eyes now,' he tells me. When I open them I find we're on the other side of the fence.

'But how?'

Sebastian smiles at my astonishment. 'I told you I'm talented...' He begins to sway on his feet.

I grab his other arm to steady him. 'Are you okay?'

The smile drops from his face as he touches a finger to his nose to find it bleeding. 'I'll be fine in a bit. We should keep moving though.'

I keep a hold of his arm to help him keep upright as we move towards the river. It scares me how pale his skin has gone and how much he struggles to walk. His shoulders are slouched over and his skin has become ice cold.

We're nearly back at the river when Sebastian stops. He walks purposefully to the edge of the last building, where he is shielded from the view of the bridge. As he peers around the corner, he swears under his breath.

I move up next to him and take a look myself, but I can't see anything other than a large open square that looks onto the darkened river.

'What's wrong?' I ask Sebastian, stepping back beside him.

'There's a whole unit of recruiters on the bridge waiting for us.'

'Really? I can't see the bridge because it's shielded from untalents,' I explain. 'What should we do?'

Sebastian swears again and takes another look at the bridge. 'We'll have to get as close to the river as possible, then I'll take us across.'

'You struggled just moving me past the fence before. How will you take me across a river that wide?'

'It will be fine,' he says.

'Surely we could go to a different spot by the river to try?'

Sebastian shakes his head. 'If we don't make it across we need the bridge to land on, otherwise we'll both drown in the river.'

'This is crazy,' I say. 'Can't we wait here until they're gone?'

'No, we can't. You can't stay here any longer and I won't have you end up like my mum. This place is not safe for you.'

'Is East Hope any safer? They think I'm a level one and plan to move me to the west. The only reason they haven't found me already is because the GPS on my cuff has been deactivated, and that will only last until tomorrow.'

'You won't get the help you need in the west. The east is our only option. We'll deal with your cuff once we're there.'

I nod and face the square. 'How do we do this?'

'We're going to have to run as close to the bridge as we can get. Then when I yell, "Now," you need to stop as still as you can and close your eyes so I can transport us to the other side.'

'And you think this will work?'

Sebastian huffs out a long breath before he responds, it billows out like a small pocket of steam in the frosty air around us. 'It's our only chance, so it has to.'

I take a hold of his hand and squeeze it. 'If anything happens...'

'I won't let it,' he replies, squeezing my hand back. He glances around the corner to look at the bridge one last time. 'Are you ready?'

'Yes,' I respond, my voice quieter and less certain than I'd intended.

'Okay, run!'

He launches himself around the corner pulling me with him. The river flows steadily before us and I push myself to run faster, to try and keep up with him as we sprint towards the bridge that only Sebastian can see.

Our feet slap loudly against the concrete ground and the muscles in my legs burn, as I will them to move as fast as they can through the cold night air. My lungs sting, allowing only shallow, frosty gasps down my narrowing throat.

There's shouting up ahead coming from the invisible bridge, and one by one, recruiters emerge by the shore, as though popping into existence from thin air. They are already running as they appear and their feet thunder across the pavement as the group of them descend on us.

'Now!' Sebastian yells. He stops running and I jarringly halt next to him. I try to become as still as possible as I shut my eyes and wait for the biting cold that tells me we're gone. But the cold doesn't come, and the pounding footsteps sound closer and closer.

After several moments, I open my eyes and turn to Sebastian to see what's going on, but as I do he disappears. His hand vanishes from mine and I am left completely alone.

Before I can consider running from the recruiters, or even lifting my hands in surrender, I feel a sharp pain in my arm. I look down and see a dart sticking out of my skin. I wrench the thing out quickly, but already I can feel its effects as my world becomes distorted.

A man approaches me and I throw my arms out, attempting to shove him away, but several others grab hold of me roughly. I kick and scream, and try to get them off of me, but they're all so strong and my vision is becoming more and more blurred.

A set of hands grab my wrists like manacles and I glare up at a burly woman who stands before me. I desperately try to escape from her grasp, but her hands feel as firm as iron. Her face lurches in and out of focus as I struggle.

'You can't do this,' I slur, my tongue feeling heavy in my mouth. 'Where are you taking me?'

I fail to catch her answer though, as the edges of my vision begin to blacken and my world plunges into darkness.

～

END OF BOOK TWO

❧

Continue in book 3: Fractured
Available here!

ACKNOWLEDGMENTS

I would like to express my gratitude to you, the reader. You are the reason I write and I am so pleased you enjoyed *Tainted* and decided to continue with Elle's story in *Talented*. I hope you have enjoyed reading both books as much as I enjoyed writing them.

Thank you to everyone who has posted reviews and used social media to help promote the series. I appreciate each and every review and post, and my success is in large part a result of your endorsement.

I wish to thank my friends who have read and loved The ARC series. Your enthusiasm is contagious and you are the best advocates for my work.

This book would not have been possible without the encouragement of my family. I am so lucky to have the support of such amazing individuals.

Finally, to Pete, your contribution has been immeasurable. You inspire me to be a better writer each and every day—not to mention, when my writing sucks you fix it!

ALSO BY ALEXANDRA MOODY

ABOUT THE AUTHOR

ALEXANDRA MOODY is an Australian author. She studied Law and Commerce in her hometown, Adelaide, before going on to spend several years living abroad in Canada and the UK. She is a serious dog-lover, double-black-diamond snowboarder and has a love/hate relationship with the gym.

Never miss a release!
Sign up at: www.subscribepage.com/TheARCsubscribe

For more information:
www.alexandramoody.com
info@alexandramoody.com

Made in the USA
San Bernardino, CA
23 February 2019